THE SHERWOOD MYSTERIES

The Shadow in the Bell Tower

JP DARCEY

THE
SHERWOOD
MYSTERIES

JP DARCEY

Printed in the United States of America	
Library of Congress Control Number:	0-9000000-0-0
ISBN: Softcover	978-1-964331-01-0
e-Book	0-9000000-0-0

Republished by: JP Darcey Mysteries

Publication Date: April 4, 2024

To order copies of this book, contact:
JP Darcey Mysteries
Phone:
inquiry@jpdarceymysteries.com

www.jpdarceymysteries.com

CONTENTS

This book is dedicated to my three grand-daughters
Ashliegh, Saffron and Georgia Bisiker.

Acknowledgments

A special thanks to Paul Howard, the best critic one could ask for. He read my early manuscript and gave me the thumbs up and said he wanted to read more.

I also wish to give thanks to Ian Wynne, GM for the hotel where I got my first job in Ireland. Also, Raymond Hirst and his daughter Erin and Connal O'hare for their support and reviews.

And finally, my family, my father and mother, my 2 Children Michael and Christopher and their families. My two sisters Rosemary and Kate and anyone I may have missed that have offered support in my writing this book. Thank you all!

JP
Darcey
Mysteries

CHAPTER ONE

The Church On The Hill

The girl walked to the edge of the village towards the ancient church. She was a lone figure on an empty street.

There aren't many people around, she thought, I hope Joan turns up.

She was on her way to choir practice at the church it was a weekly event held on a Thursday evening.

As she drew nearer to the building its bell tower appeared to be reaching towards the star lit sky before it carelessly threw its shadow on the old graves below. It was situated at the top of a hill. Stone steps, weathered and worn with age climbed up to the church from a gated porch at the roadside. A low wall with an iron railing attached to it, ran at the side of the steps to help the not so fit reach the top.

When she arrived at the porch gate she stood at the roadside and waited for her best friend Joan Parsons. She hugged herself to keep warm in the cool September air and impatiently kicked at the dirt on the ground as she casually pushed back her unruly curls. A favourite song came into her head, so she quietly hummed the tune to break the still silence. The tune was *A Hard Days Night*, the latest hit song by *The Beatles*.

Why couldn't her hair be straighter like Joan's, she thought, as she still tried to control her curls. She was becoming more concerned about her appearance now that she was thirteen.

Christine Danvers, also known as Chrissy, by friends and family, was tall for her age. She was of medium build, with shoulder length, dark brown hair. She had large brown eyes, a roundish face and a pert nose. She wasn't attractive like her friend, but she was what you would call cute and maybe even regarded as pretty by some.

As Chrissy continued to hum her tune, she thought how nice it would be to go and see The Beatles, even though she knew it would probably never happen.

Suddenly Chrissy jumped, her silent pondering had been disturbed by Joan's familiar voice.

"What are you day-dreaming about, Danvers?" "Oh, I wish you'd stop sneaking up on me like that" she gasped, her heart still pounding from the sudden fright.

"Have you been waiting long?"

"No!" said Chrissy as she casually stretched, now that she was back in the real world.

She yawned and looked upwards. Something in the tower had just caught her eye.

"Did you see what I just saw?" whispered Chrissy. "What do you mean did I see what you just saw?

What's that imagination of yours conjuring up now?" "No, I mean it. I saw something move in the bell tower. A shape passed by the window, like a white shadowy shape." explained Chrissy.

Joan stared at the tower where Chrissy was pointing.

"See! There it is again. You must have seen it." "I'm not quite sure. Maybe I did see something,"

Joan appeared puzzled. "Oh, come on Chrissy you've even got me imagining things now. Get your mind back in gear, here comes the vicar."

"Good evening, Reverend Timas," the girls chorused, as though they were already in choir practice.

"Good evening, young ladies."

Reverend Timas was a tall, slim, middle aged man with thin lips and a stern face. His everyday attire which he now wore consisted of a cassock that buttoned up the front and a long black cape. The robes he wore for church services were more regal. They were made out of gold and white fabric, and embroidered with gold thread.

Reverend Timas asked that his parishioners call him Reverend Timas. Although he was an approachable man he felt the name vicar was too informal for his station in life.

"Where is the rest of the choir, ladies?"

"There's only the two of us tonight sir," said Joan. "Oh well, two is better than none. Come on then, let's get started. I have to visit Colonel Darcy later on this evening." He said, as he opened the porch gates and climbed up the steps two at a time.

The girls followed and hurried to keep up. They clutched at the cold iron railing to keep their balance. The Reverend's cape flowed wildly behind him in the wind, giving him the appearance of a large black crow in flight.

What a sight this would look to a stranger standing on the street below, thought Chrissy. A spectre in black leading two girls up to the church, in the dark! She giggled.

"What's up with you now?" whispered Joan.

"I think I'll ask the vicar if I can borrow his black cape for the Halloween party. I can dress up as Batman."

"Shush! He'll hear you." Joan whispered again. "Is

there anything the matter ladies?" Reverend Timas asked.

He had just reached the top step and turned back towards the girls.

Chrissy tried hard not to laugh. "No, Reverend Timas," she giggled.

Reverend Timas shook his head and sighed, then turned back towards the church. He pulled a large key from a pocket in his cloak and put it of the keyhole in the church door. The key creaked and groaned in the rusty lock.

"Come on ladies."

He beckoned to them as he opened the heavy door and walked into the outer porch of the church.

Chrissy shivered when she entered. The porch was cold, musty, and smelt damp. She hugged herself as she watched Reverend Timas retrieve another key and a lantern from a ledge near the inner door to the church.

"What's the lantern for sir?" asked Joan.

"The electrical wiring in the church is old, and I don't feel it's safe to leave the power turned on when there is no one here. I have to go to the back of the church to turn on the main electrical switch."

He lit the lantern, unlocked the inner door, and headed to the back of the church.

"Ohhh! Does he ever look spooky!" whispered Chrissy.

"He looks as though he's floating in the lantern light."

"Shut up! He'll hear you. Can't you be serious about anything?" snapped Joan.

"Of course I can. It's not my fault people don't take me seriously," Chrissy sighed.

Chrissy hung her head and looked down at her feet. She wandered why people never took her seriously. Was it because she had an overactive imagination? Unfortunately it did get her into trouble at times.

The memory of the time she saw Mr. Dickson from the farm next door to her house, came into her head. Mr. Dickson was pushing a large plastic sack under a bush. She had thought that the butcher's dog was in the sack. The dog had disappeared two days earlier.

Mr. Dickson didn't like other people's dogs on his farm. He had shot at dogs before. So Chrissy convinced her father that Mr. Dickson had probably done away with the butcher's dog, put it in the sack, and pushed it under the bush.

Chrissy's father had gone to see Mr. Dickson and insisted that he show him what was in the sack, or he would call the police.

When Mr. Dickson eventually opened the sack and revealed a large garden gnome Chrissy knew she was in deep trouble. She was right, she wasn't allowed out with her friends for a week.

The gnome had been a surprise gift for Mrs. Dickson, but it wasn't a surprise anymore. Mrs. Dickson had watched as the sack was being opened.

The bright lights glowing from the large chandeliers in the church suddenly brought Chrissy back to the present.

"Come on day dreamer," said Joan.

"Okay, I'm coming, Miss Bossy," Chrissy snapped, as she followed her friend into the church.

Kirkby village church was about eight hundred years old. Its sturdy stone walls were made out of local quarried stone that had been formed into large blocks.

The inside of the magnificent building always amazed Chrissy. Huge stone slabs covered the floors inside the church. In the aisles between the pews, a worn red carpet covered the stones. Beneath the stone floors lay the crypts that held the remains of long dead noblemen, who now lay peacefully in their ancient stone coffins.

At the front of the church stood a massive stained glass window that overlooked the church alter. The alter was adorned with fresh flowers and a large golden cross. A large pipe organ stood towards the back of the church, its massive pipes reached to the ceiling and appeared to be bursting through the roof like rockets waiting a launch instruction.

Chrissy sneezed! The pungent odour from the Beeswax polish used on the pews tickled her nose.

"Bless you," said Reverend Timas who had just appeared from the back of the church. "Come on ladies, let's get started". He ushered the girls into the pews in front of the pipe organ.

Chrissy obediently took her seat next to Joan, but instead of concentrating on choir practice, his thoughts carelessly wondered back to the shadow in the bell tower.

"Excuse me, Reverend Timas," interrupted Chrissy. "Do you believe in ghosts?"

The Reverend was surprised by Chrissy's question but he answered with enthusiasm.

"I keep an open mind young lady, even though I have never actually seen one. Mind you a strange thing did happen just the other week, when my spectacles went missing."

"Oh what happened, do tell us." Chrissy was bursting with excitement.

Reverend Timas proceeded to tell the girls about the night he had been going over Sunday's hymns with the organist. After the meeting, he found he had misplaced his spectacles. He searched for them for a while then decided he would continue the search the next day. It was getting late and he had no need of them that night.

The following day he continued his search. He was at the back of the church, behind the organ when he heard a deep voice coming from the bell tower. The voice told him to look behind him on the steps to the tower, which he did, and there were his spectacles.

"To this day I cannot explain this occurrence," said Reverend Timas.

Chrissy sat rigid in her seat, her mouth fell open. She couldn't wait for choir practice to end so she could leave the church and its bodyless voices. But then, as usual, curiosity got the better of her. She could smell a mystery. She had to find out more.

At the end of choir practice, Chrissy eagerly began questioning Joan. She had to know what she thought about the vicar's mysterious voice.

"Do you believe in ghosts?" Chrissy asked. "I don't really know," said Joan.

"Do you think what the vicar told us was true?" "I don't know." Joan snapped. She was losing patience with Chrissy. "Maybe he just wanted to scare us so we would stop our stupid giggling. Why don't you ask him?"

"I will," Chrissy announced. "You're not?" gasped Joan. "I am."

Chrissy liked a challenge.

"Okay. He goes over the hymns with the organist tomorrow night. We'll catch him at the gate before he goes up to the church. You can ask him then."

By this time Joan was already half way down the street.

Joan lived two farmhouses down from Chrissy, on the opposite side of the road. The girl's fathers were both farmers.

"I've got homework to do and so have you. I'll see you in the morning on the school bus," Joan shouted back.

"Yuck! Homework! Who could get excited about homework," moaned Chrissy.

Chrissy's shoulders slouched when she crossed the road to her house. Life suddenly felt boring again. Then she heard the contented mooing of the cows in the shed nearby. The sound of the cows and the sweet smell of the hay always made her feel better. There was a spring in her step again when she walked round the side of the house.

"Goodnight, cows!" she said. "See you in the morning."

CHAPTER TWO

The Shadow In The Bell Tower

The following evening Chrissy and Joan met by the church porch gate at the time they had previously arranged. While they waited for Reverend Timas Chrissy stared intently at the bell tower window. "Come on Joan let's look at the bell tower. Maybe we might see something," urged Chrissy.

As if on cue something passed by the tower window.

"There! Did you see it this time?"

"I definitely did. A white shape passed by the window," shrieked Joan. "What could it be?"

Chrissy started imagining all sorts of things. She saw huge white shapes popping up all over the churchyard. They were like restless spirits roaming the churchyard on an endless quest for eternal peace. The spirits were coming towards her, what should she do.................

"What are you two young ladies doing here tonight?"

Chrissy jumped, she was startled back to reality. Her restless spirits disappeared as quickly as they had appeared. Instead, they were replaced by Reverend Timas who had appeared to have come from nowhere.

"Reverend Timas! You gave me such a fright," panted Chrissy. "Look at the bell tower window, sir." "And what am I looking for?" asked Reverend Timas sternly.

"Just a little while ago a white shadowy shape moved past the window sir," explained Chrissy.

"I'm afraid I only see darkness," said Reverend Timas. "Is that wild imagination of yours playing tricks on you again, Christine?"

"I don't think so Reverend Timas," interrupted Joan. "I saw it too. I'm sure I did.

"Reverend Timas that story you told us last night..... the one about your spectacles going missing was it true?" spluttered Chrissy.

"Ladies, I know my story may have sounded unbelievable but it was absolutely true. There are many mysteries in life we don't understand."

"Who do you think spoke to you?" asked Chrissy. "I have no idea, it was a faceless voice. It's one of those mysteries."

"Aren't you curious?" asked Chrissy.

"No. If I am supposed to find out whose voice it was, I will find out when the time is right."

"How do you know when the time is right?" asked Chrissy.

Reverend Timas was starting to get annoyed at Chrissy's constant questions.

"Christine! You ask too many questions. Now young ladies I must be going. Mrs. Poole will be waiting."

Reverend Timas opened the porch gate and climbed the steps to the church. His cape flowed behind him in the breeze like the large black crow taking flight again.

Chrissy continued to watch while he disappeared into the church in a black cloud. She could see the church lights shining through the arched windows. She hadn't noticed them before.

Mrs. Poole must be in the church already, thought Chrissy. Was that thing in the bell tower while Mrs. Poole was alone in the church? Chrissy shivered at the thought.

Again Chrissy was startled from her deep thoughts, this time by a loud noise coming from the other side of the church. It sounded like something or someone had dropped from the bell tower onto the grass. Then she heard a sound like someone was running through the grass and the bushes. Then there was silence. a deadly silence. She stared at Joan in disbelief.

"This merits an investigation," announced Joan. "There is something strange going on here."

"Oh, Joan!" cried Chrissy her fearless enthusiasm returning. "I was waiting for you to say that."

"As it's Saturday tomorrow," said Joan. "We can start our investigations in the morning."

Chrissy was so excited about the prospect of an adventure she couldn't stop herself from hugging Joan.

"Chrissy stop it. You'll knock me down you silly hound."

"Joan, do you think we should tell someone? Like maybe an adult?" asked Chrissy.

"Reverend Timas didn't believe us when we told him about the mysterious moving shadow in the bel tower why should any other adult?" stated Joan. "We have to investigate first. We have to find out what it was we saw in the bell tower. It appears to me that something or someone may be trying to frighten people away from the church at night."

"Why?" asked Chrissy.

"That's what we have got to find out," Joan said impatiently.

"Maybe the voice Reverend Timas heard coming from inside the bell tower has something to do with the mysterious shadow we have been seeing up there," whispered Chrissy.

"I think you're right. Anyway, we'll see what we can find out tomorrow."

The girls turned round and set off back down the street towards home.

The village of Kirkby only had one main street. It ran through the centre of the village for about a mile and a half. At one end of the street stood the shop and post office and at the other end, stood the church on the hill. In the middle was the public house, The Fox & Hare.

The rest of the street consisted of farmhouses of various shapes and sizes and a row of elderly people's cottages near the church. The girls lived between The Fox & Hare and the and post office.

Chrissy loved this little village in the county of Nottinghamshire. The district was full of historic sites and large stately homes that once belonged to the local gentry and former Dukes of Nottinghamshire. Now most of the large houses were open for the public to view, to help pay for their upkeep.

Chrissy had listened many times to the interesting tales that were told by the old folk of the district. Tales of days gone by, legends which became more exciting each time they were told, especially those of Robin Hood and his merry men.

Kirkby was situated on what was once part of Sherwood Forest, the hideout of Robin Hood and his men. Now there were only a few hundred acres of Sherwood Forest left. The remaining forest was about fifteen miles away from the village of Kirkby.

Chrissy, her father, her mother, and her two older sisters, Susan and Elizabeth, had moved to Kirkby five years earlier. Her mother had left them three years after their move.

Chrissy had arrived home from school one day to find her mother had taken her belongings and moved out. She had written a note saying that she was tired of the hard work and long hours running the farm and taking care of the house. A year after that Chrissy's parents divorced and a few months later, her mother met someone new and remarried.

Chrissy's mother had asked Chrissy and her sisters if they wanted to live with her in her new home, but they had said no. Chrissy wanted to stay with her father in the village she had grown to love. She wanted her mother to come home to her family and their home but it wasn't to be.

Her friendship with Joan had filled part of the emptiness in her life that was there because of her mother's absence but she found her mind would wonder when it was only occupied with everyday thoughts and deeds. She would conjure up all kind of ideas in her head to take her away from reality. That's how she came to develop the vivid imagination she now possessed.

Now Chrissy had a real adventure to occupy her thoughts. How would she sleep tonight? She couldn't wait for the morning.

CHAPTER THREE

The Shed In The Woods

Chrissy walked into the kitchen the next morning to find her father sitting at the table eating his breakfast.

"Hello, Dad. Have you already fed the cows?" "Good morning, lass. Yes I have fed the cows, I was out in the cow shed while you were still tucked up in bed snoring," said Sam Danvers.

Sam loved working outside in the fresh air and he loved his life as a farmer. He had once worked in the local coal mines. He still remembered the dust, stale air, and gloomy darkness of the mines.

Sam was a tall, lean man in his forties. He had dark brown wavy hair that was now greying at the sides.

"And what are you up to today?" He asked. "Staying out of trouble I hope."

"Of course," said Chrissy innocently. "Joan and I are just going out for a walk."

Chrissy didn't like to tell her father too much. She thought he worried unnecessarily about what she might get up to, or what trouble she might get into.

"You should be okay with Joan," he said. "She's a smart lass. Let's hope some of that rubs off on you. Hey Chrissy!"

"Oh, Dad, I don't always get in trouble."

Sam smiled and patted his daughter on the head like she was still a little girl. Chrissy frowned. Although she was the youngest in the family, she was now a teenager. She wished people would treat her like one.

"I'd better be off," said Sam as he got up from the table. He put his dishes in the sink and got his coat from a hook by the kitchen door.

"I'll see you at dinnertime then, shall I?"

Sam walked out the door into the yard before waiting for an answer from Chrissy.

"I should think so," shouted Chrissy as the kitchen door closed.

As soon as her father had gone she hurried over to the kitchen cupboard to get the breakfast cereal but before she could get herself a bowl she heard voices in the yard.

Oh no thought Chrissy. I think Dad must have run into Joan in the yard, she musn't tell Dad that we are investigating round the churchyard.

With the box of cereal still in her hands she rushed out through the kitchen door into the yard.

"Joan you're here at last," gasped Chrissy.

She grabbed Joan's arm and pulled her back towards the house.

A puzzled Joan shouted back to Chrissy's father. "See you later, Mr. Danvers."

"Yeh, see you later, Dad," shouted Chrissy, as she pushed Joan into the kitchen.

"What was all that about?" cried Joan.

"I didn't want you to tell my dad we were doing some investigating round the churchyard." Chrissy was puffing and panting from the excitement. "You know how he worries about what I get up too. Besides, you said we shouldn't tell any adults anything yet."

"You're right. They wouldn't understand," said Joan as a quizzical look came over her face.

"Why are you looking at me like that?" asked Chrissy.

"What's this on your hair?"

Joan reached up and touched Chrissy's forehead. "This?"

Chrissy had sticky tape taped across her fringe, and the back and sides of her hair.

"It's sellotape," she replied indignantly.

"Why on earth have you got sellotape plastered across your hair?"

"My hair's not straight like yours. I put sellotape on to straighten it after I wash it. I saw it in a magazine."

"You look like a misplaced parcel," laughed Joan. "Ha! Ha! At least I'll be a misplaced parcel with straight hair," moaned Chrissy.

"Oh Christine, you are a case. Come on, you're not even dressed yet. We don't want to lose any valuable investigating time."

Chrissy gulped down a bowl of cereal and then rushed upstairs to get dressed. When she reached her bedroom on the third floor she ran over to her dressing table and fumbled messily through her clothes. She pulled out an old pair of jeans and a heavy red jumper.

She got dressed quickly as it was cold in her attic

bedroom. Central heating was a luxury and only the new houses which were built for the wealthier people were equipped with this luxury.

Fifteen minutes later the girls were outside on the street. It was a lovely sunny September morning. Chrissy breathed in the fresh country air as they made their way through the village to the church.

Many of the villagers were out in their gardens raking up leaves. The girls waved to them as they passed by. But when they got closer to the church porch gate they made sure no one was watching them. Quickly they looked up and down the street before they opened the gate and scrambled up the steps. They ran up to the church and stayed close to the walls so they wouldn't be seen from the street below. Cautiously they edged their way round to the other side of the church.

The grass was long and still damp from the morning dew. By the time they had reached their intended destination the bottom of their jeans were wet and their shoes squelched from the moisture that had got inside them.

When Chrissy looked towards the bell tower she noticed that the grass on the ground beneath the tower had recently been flattened down. A rope hung halfway down the wall from the tower window.

"Someone must have dropped down here," said Joan as she crouched down by the flattened grass.

"Look!" cried Chrissy. "There's a trail of trampled grass leading into the woods."

Chrissy was anxious to see where the trail led, so without another word she took off towards the woods.

"Come on Joan let's go," she shouted as she ran at full speed through the churchyard.

She was so excited she didn't see the old broken gravestone that was sticking out of the ground.

Before Chrissy knew it she had tripped and was lying face down on the soft, damp grass.

"I'd better go first," said Joan as she helped Chrissy to her feet. "I'm not as clumsy as you."

"I'm not clumsy," moaned Chrissy who was a little stunned and annoyed at her own stupidity. "But I'll let you go first anyway."

"Hang on a minute," said Joan. She was still holding onto Chrissy's arm. "These woods are supposed to be haunted by an old monk. Hundreds of years ago there used to be a monastery where the church is now."

"Oh! Come on Joan. Everyone knows ghosts don't come out in the daytime. Let's go."

Chrissy pushed Joan forward, she wanted to get going. Now eager with anticipation, the girls followed the trail of trampled grass into the woods. Carefully stepping over old tree stumps and edging round large tree trunks. Until they came to a clearing in the trees, in the middle of the clearing stood a shed.

"Look over there!" cried Joan. "There's an old shed. Why would there be a shed here? I've lived in these parts all my life, I didn't know about any sheds in these woods."

"Have you been through here often?" asked Chrissy.

Joan now whispered. "No. Like I said, the woods are supposed to be haunted."

"Let's have a look," Chrissy whispered back.

"We better be careful. There might be someone in there."

Chrissy held on to Joan as they crept up to the shed and slowly inched round to the other side. There they found an old door precariously hanging from its rusty hinges. The door looked as though it was just about ready to fall to the ground. Cautiously Joan walked up to the door and lifted it up so she could pull it open.

Chrissy took hold of Joan's arm again and nervously peeked into the shed. She squinted until her eyes got accustomed to the lack of light inside.

The first thing Chrissy noticed was a wooden platform attached to the far wall. On it was a pillow and a blanket.

Next to the platform was a box that contained some tins of food, a plate, and various kitchen utensils. To her right in the corner of the shed, stood a garden fork and an empty burlap sack.

"Someone was here recently," whispered Joan as she picked up the plate from the box on the floor. "This plate has fairly fresh food on it."

Joan's verbal observations suddenly abruptly stopped. She was still and silent as if she had been frozen in time. Before Chrissy knew what was happening Joan clamped her hand over her mouth.

"Shush! I can hear something," whispered Joan.

Chrissy listened. She could hear a rustling sound in the trees behind them. Joan grabbed her hand and roughly pulled her out of the shed. She ran to the trees in front of them and pulled Chrissy behind a large oak tree.

"Stand there and keep quiet," she whispered as she pressed Chrissy's body up against the rough bark on the tree trunk.

Chrissy stood rigid, she didn't move, she barely breathed and the seconds seemed to turn into endless minutes. Then she began to get fidgety, she wasn't one for staying still very long and her curious nature was urging her to see what was going on. Without a word to Joan she slowly inched her way back round the tree. She was just in time to see a man disappear inside the shed.

"It's an ordinary man! It's not a ghost." Chrissy whispered as she moved back towards an alarmed Joan.

Chrissy noticed that the man had been wearing a faded brown tweed jacket and brown corduroy trousers. He appeared to be in his late twenties, or early thirties. His hair was not yet greying like her father's hair was.

"Keep your voice down," whispered Joan. "We don't want him to know we are here. I saw a large knife sticking out from underneath that blanket. He may be dangerous."

Chrissy suddenly felt scared again. Joan was right. If the man was hiding for some reason, he might be dangerous.

The girls waited in silence for a while longer until they decided that it was save to move. The man appeared to be staying in the shed.

After listening hard for any unusual sounds they quietly tiptoed away from their sanctuary. Then they ran and didn't stop running until they had reached the fence at the edge of the woods. They hastily climbed the fence into the field next to the woods and raced across the field to the gate at the other end and climbed over the gate to the road.

"We should go and talk to old Tom," gasped Joan. "He knows more than anyone about the church and the village."

"You mean he might know about the shed and why it is there?" cried Chrissy still trying to catch her breath.

"Yes!"

"You said we shouldn't tell any adults yet," she panted.

"Old Tom won't tell anyone if we ask him not to. He's a nice old chap and he likes hearing about a good mystery."

Now that Chrissy was away from the immediate danger of the stranger and his dangerous knife, her enthusiasm returned. Her heart beat loudly in her chest. She was excited about the thought of what could be a very interesting and exciting adventure. Eagerly she followed Joan back into the village to old Tom Peter's cottage.

Old Tom Peters

The girls found old Tom in his garden. He was using his walking stick to pick out potatoes from the loosened earth. Old Tom was in his eighties but he still managed to grow a few potatoes and vegetables for himself.

The cottage where Tom Peters lived was one of four that had been built by the old squire, Edward Langford. Edward Langford and his family had been local wealthy landowners. They had once owned Kirkby Manor and the old Squire had built the cottages for the retired farm hands who had worked his land.

It was common knowledge in the district that the surviving members of Edward Langford's family were now poor. Kirkby Manor and the land had been sold shortly after the old Squires death. The manor was now a retirement home.

All the cottages had been sold but one, old Toms.

Tom's cottage had been deeded to him when the old Squire had died.

"Hello Mr. Peters! How are you today?" shouted Joan.

Joan whispered to Chrissy. "He doesn't hear very well."

"Well bless me, if it isn't young Joan Parsons. How's your father, lass?" old Tom shouted back.

Joan whispered again to Chrissy. "Old Tom used to do odd jobs for my dad."

"He's very well, thank you, Mr. Peters."

"Who's that with you, lass?" shouted old Tom. "Is that young, Chrissy Danvers? I saw her dad t' other day at market."

"Yes Mr. Peters, it's me, Chrissy Danvers. How are you?" shouted Chrissy.

"Aye, I still like to go to market once a week on the bus," old Tom said to himself more than to the girls. "Nice chap, your dad."

"Can we have a word with you, Mr. Peters?" shouted Joan. "We wanted to know if you knew anything about the old shed in the church woods."

"Ohh! Aye I do lass. What do you want to know?" he asked. "By the way, there's no need to shout, I can still hear. Come into the cottage and we'll have a talk."

Chrissy laughed quietly at old Tom's denial of having poor hearing.

"Would you lasses like a glass of lemonade?" he asked as he ushered the girls into the cottage.

"Thank you, Mr. Peters, we'd love some," said Chrissy who didn't like to say no to any free refreshments.

Old Tom motioned for the girls to sit down by the fire on an old faded green couch. As Chrissy sat down she made her usual curious observations round the room. Dried logs crackled and spluttered in the grate. The fire spread a warm glow across the kitchen. She could see that the only other light in the room was from a small window above the kitchen sink. Faded green gingham curtains hung in the window. The porcelain sink was stained and cracked from many years of use. On the draining board stood a solitary cup and a large plate, a reminder that there was now just one lonely individual occupying the cottage. Tom's wife had died some years past.

At one time the kitchens in these cottages were not only used for cooking and eating, but also for everyday living. There was a room at the front of the house but that was only used on Sundays and special occasions.

Tom's front room was probably never used now.

As old Tom reached for two glasses from the cabinet by the sink, Chrissy looked at the faded green couch she and Joan were sitting on.

It's obviously seen better days, she thought, most likely a cast off from the old manor.

The couch looked as though it had once been of rich, emerald green velvet. She could still see patches of its true colour in the crevices between the cushions. "I'll be back in a jiffy," muttered old Tom as he disappeared outside.

Chrissy looked at Joan and smiled. "He's quite a character, isn't he?" she said.

Old Tom returned with a large blue porcelain jug, his hand shook as he poured the lemonade into the glasses and carried them over to the girls. The glasses were only two thirds full by the time they reached their destination, after their shaky journey across the kitchen.

"Aren't you having a drink, Mr. Peters?" asked Joan, as old Tom sat himself in a creaky rocking chair opposite the couch.

"No lass, not right now. I'm curious to know what you want to talk to me about?" he asked, as he pulled out a pipe from his top pocket.

He banged the pipe on the grate in the fireplace to

remove the burnt tobacco.

Without any hesitation Chrissy started spluttering out their story about the shadow in the bell tower and the shed in the woods.

"Hang on a minute, lass. You're talking too fast," cried Tom. "Me hearin's not that good anymore."

"Sorry Mr. Peters," interrupted Joan. "I'll tell the story."

Joan frowned at Chrissy and then continued to tell old Tom about the last couple of days, while he filled his pipe from a tobacco pouch he had picked up from the mantle shelf. He didn't appear to be listening to Joan until he had lit his pipe and settled back in his chair. A pungent cloud of smoke rose to the ceiling.

"What do you think Mr. Peters?" Joan asked when she had finished telling their story.

"I heard tell that Jack Langford lived in those woods for a while. Some years back it was," he said.

"Why?" asked Chrissy.

"It's a long story, lass. I'll try and tell it best I can.

Jack Langford was the squire's eldest son."

Old Tom appeared to be in deep thought recalling

the story.

"You know, Mr. Edward Langford that once owned Kirkby Manor?" he recalled.

"Yes, we've heard the story," replied Joan.

"Well Jack was a bad sort. He was a drinker and a gambler when he was just a young man, from what I can recall. He treated us workers like dirt, the ones that worked in the house and on the land. He had no respect for us."

The story went that Edward Langford wasn't too happy about leaving the manor and the land to Jack. He believed that Jack would lose the estate in a card game, or sell it for gambling money. So he had his Will changed. It was changed so that when he died, his youngest son Harry would get the house and the land.

"Harry Langford is still alive, isn't he?" Joan enquired.

"Aye that's right lass."

"But I heard the old manor house was now a retirement home," interrupted Chrissy.

"Aye, it is lass."

Old Tom continued the story.

When the old squire died and Jack discovered his

brother Harry had been left the estate, Jack was very angry. At first he took his anger out on his wife, Mary. He made her life miserable, fighting with her over the least little thing until she could take no more of it. She was afraid of Jack and feared for her safety and the safety of their son, Peter. Finally she decided to leave him and so she took Peter and moved away from the district. She didn't let anyone know where she was going for fear of Jack finding her.

His wife leaving him made Jack even angrier. Even though he had never really cared for his wife, as it had been an arranged marriage for money, he didn't like the idea of her taking his son.

He became unreasonable, rebellious, and hard to live with. He spent money like there was no tomorrow.

He bought expensive foods from grocery suppliers and bottles of wine and liquor from the brewery. He had all the bills sent up to the manor house for his brother to pay.

Jack then went down to London to stay at the club where his father still had a membership. At the club he forged his father's signature and cashed cheques for large amounts of money. He ordered more expensive food and drink gambling his days away.

While Jack was in London, Harry had discovered that valuable items were missing from the house, paintings and precious jewellery that had been in the family for generations. Expensive silver pieces had also disappeared and stock certificates were missing from the safe in the house.

Harry suspected Jack had a hand in this. He tried to contact his brother at the London Club but he discovered that the day before, the club had become aware of old Mr. Langford's death. Jack had then been thrown out on the streets. The club chairman told Harry he would be sending him Jack's bills.

The story continued. After Harry had cleared his brother's debts, the estate's bank accounts were practically empty. Harry had to sell all the valuable items that were left, to pay the household bills and the farm workers. By this time Harry realised they could no longer afford to live in the manor house.

Harry and his wife Alice had to sell the house and most of the land. But they managed to keep the old hunting lodge to live in. The lodge was at the edge of the estate beside a few acres of woodland that the family had once owned.

The hunting lodge had been built years earlier by his grandfather. It was fashionable back then for a large estate to own a hunting lodge. It was a place for guests to rest after a day's hunting in the forest, instead of making their way back to the manor. The guests stayed the night at the lodge where they were entertained by their host.

"Aye, they still live in the hunting lodge today," said

Tom. "Mr. Harry became a writer, but he can't write much anymore. He has arthritis real bad. Mrs. Langford is poorly as well. She has to go to the hospital at least once a week."

"What happened to Jack's wife and son?" asked Joan.

"Nobody knows, they still don't know to this day. Aye, Peter Langford the son would be in his early thirties now. He was only a little-un when this all happened."

"Aye, Mr. Harry and his wife are in a sorry state," continued Tom. "Poor as church mice they do say. There's not much money left to pay for their needs and keep t'old lodge in good repair. Although the lodge isn't as big as the manor house, it's still quite a big house."

"Did they ever find Jack and the paintings and what about the precious jewellery and all the other things that were missing?" asked Chrissy. "Do they think he might have sold them? Or that he might have hidden them somewhere in the village?"

"They don't know lass. People say they tried to find em through antique dealers and the stock certificates through the banks. But they couldn't find anything."

"Well what's all this got to do with the shed in the woods and the shadow in the bell tower?" asked Joan.

A hot shard of wood fell from the fire and burnt out on the stone floor. Old Tom continued to puff on his pipe. Chrissy noticed that a black patch had formed on the ceiling above the rocking chair. Most likely from many years of pipe smoke rising up to the same spot, she thought.

"The shed in the woods used be a woodman's shed many, many years ago," Tom continued. "They found out that Mr. Jack had lived there after he got thrown out of the club in London. That's after he had lived for a while at t' old Fox & Hare public house, down the road. He got thrown out of there as well for not paying his bills."

"He sounds like a real bad sort," said Chrissy thoughtfully.

"Aye lass, he was that and strange he was. He used to be seen wandering up and down the street in the middle of the night.

It scared some folks and that's when they realised he must have been still living somewhere local. That's when they thought he was probably hiding in t'old woodman's shed. It's the only place he could have stayed."

"How come I never knew about the shed in the woods, Mr. Peters?" asked Joan.

"Villagers didn't want the children going up near them woods back then. We thought Mr. Jack had gone mad, crazy in t'head like. Folk didn't know what he might do to anyone he saw in them woods. So they kept telling the story of the monk's ghost to frighten kids away from the woods. Did your mam and dad never tell you the story lass?"

"Yes, they did," replied Joan. "A lot of people still believe the story of the monk's ghost. That's why I hadn't been in the woods before. I'd had no need to until today, and so of course that's why I didn't know about the shed."

"Did they ever tell you the story of the man they found dead by the church door, one real cold winter morning?" asked Tom. "Aye, he were frozen stiff he was. That was another story that frightened the kids away from the churchyard and the woods."

"Yes, I think I remember a little bit about it," recalled Joan. "My mum and dad had talked about it. They weren't very old themselves when that happened."

"That was Mr. Jack they found at the church door. They say he probably knew he was going to die. So they thought he went to repent his sins at the church. Aye, he must have lived in those woods for nigh on five years afore he died."

Old Tom sat silent again, his pipe was held away from his mouth. Chrissy wondered if he had fallen asleep because his eyes were closed.

She nudged Joan.

"I think he's fallen asleep," whispered Chrissy. "No I haven't lass," said Tom suddenly like he was coming back to life again. "I was thinking." That made Chrissy jump.

"Who do you think the man hiding in the shed in the woods is, Mr. Peters?" she asked.

"I don't rightly know lass. It could be someone looking for the missing Langford treasures. Some folks think they were hidden in the churchyard. A lot of them have searched, but nobody ever found them."

"Really!" exclaimed Chrissy.

"Aye lass you never know." Tom laughed, amused by Chrissy's curiosity. "Aye, it would sure help Mr. Harry and his poor wife if someone found their missing treasures and gave em back to the poor folk."

"Maybe we should find out if that's what the man hiding in the woods is after?" suggested Joan with excitement.

Chrissy, bubbling with curiosity couldn't wait to investigate further.

"Now you two young lasses be careful." Tom wagged his finger at the girls. "That man might be dangerous. If he's hiding in them woods and looking for the treasure, he's not going to want anyone else finding out what he's up to."

Chrissy sat back and folded her arms across her chest. Of course they would be careful. We aren't children, she thought.

Joan sighed as she got up and signalled Chrissy to do the same.

"Thanks for the information and the lemonade Mr. Peters," said Joan politely. "Your story could explain a lot about what's been going on. And don't worry, we will be very careful."

"Mr. Peters," she continued. "Please don't tell anyone we were talking to you. Not until we have more information. They might stop us trying to find the treasure. They might say we are going on a wild goose chase. You know how some people think."

"Okay lass," said Tom. "But like I said, you just watch yourselves and be careful. That chap could be dangerous."

"Okay, Mr. Peters, and thanks," said Chrissy, as the girls waved their goodbyes.

The girls walked out onto the street into the bright sunlight. Chrissy grabbed Joan's arm.

"What are we going to do?" asked Chrissy. "Right now, we are going to go home for some lunch," replied Joan. "I'll have a think while I'm eating."

"We have got to find out if that man is after the Langford's treasure."

"I know, but we have got to plan this carefully. Like old Tom said, this man could be dangerous. Remember the knife? Now let's go and have lunch. I'll see you in about an hour."

Joan dashed off down the street to her house. Chrissy still stood on the spot where Joan had left her. Her mouth was wide open as if she was going to say something.

"Why do we always have to wait until later," said Chrissy out loud as she made her way down the street to her house.

CHAPTER FIVE

Harry & Alice Langford

One o'clock that afternoon, Chrissy and Joan sat in Chrissy's kitchen working out a plan of what to do next regarding the mystery man in the woods and the missing Langford's treasure.

Joan hadn't come up with any good ideas during her lunch, but they now agreed that they should definitely find out if the man hiding in the church woods was looking for the treasure. And if he were, he had no rights to it as the treasure rightfully belonged to the Langford's, not him, whoever he was.

Although Chrissy had never met Harry and Alice Langford, she was starting to feel sorry for this poor old couple who had been deprived of their home and land. Because of this they were now nearly living in poverty.

It's just not right, felt Chrissy.

"I know!" cried Joan. "We'll go and visit Mr & Mrs Langford."

"What! You mean just drop by?"

Chrissy was astonished that Joan should suggest such a thing.

"Won't they think that's strange, two kids they have never met, just turning up on their doorstep."

Joan convinced Chrissy that it would be a good idea to get to know the Langfords and find out more about Jack Langford and the missing family treasures. They would need more information to carry out their investigations properly.

"How are we going to do this without the Langfords thinking that we're on some silly wild goose chase?" asked Chrissy. "After all, old Tom did say other people had tried to find the Langford treasure without any success."

"How about we say we are doing a school project or something like that?"

"Yes! That's it! We can say we are researching the history of Kirkby Manor and its past owners," said Chrissy her enthusiasm returning in full force.

"That sounds like a great idea," Joan agreed. "We will ask what the house used to look like in those days and what style of furniture they had and what valuable *paintings* or *silver pieces* used to decorate the manor.”

"We will ask if they still have some of the items from the old manor, like old pieces of furniture or, valuable paintings or silver pieces," said Chrissy. "We can also find out if the ladies had precious jewellery that had been handed down from generation to generation and did Mrs. Langford still have any of it."

"And we can ask if we can take photographs or if they have any photographs of these items, because they would help with the presentation of our school project," announced Joan.

So it was agreed; they would visit the Langfords and secretly, but politely, get whatever information they could to help with their investigations. They would need photographs if they had to immediately identify anything they might find.

"Go and get your bike Chrissy. I'll meet you at my place in about fifteen minutes," She rushed out of Chrissy's house to go home and get her bike.

Fifteen minutes later the girls were cycling through the village in the opposite direction to the church. After they passed the post office and shop at the end of the village they started a steady climb up the hill going towards the next village. Half way up the hill the girls came to a side road with a signpost that said, Kirkby Manor.

"If we go along here for about half a mile we will

come to a fork in the road," explained Joan. "The road to the right goes to Kirkby Manor and the left leads to the hunting lodge."

"How do you know?"

"I went up to the manor house with my dad once. He was taking something up to the retirement home for the Matron."

After cycling about half a mile just as Joan had said, the girls came to the fork in the road and another signpost pointing right to Kirkby Manor. They took the left road.

Chrissy started to feel like they had been on the road for hours. Then she spotted a large house some distance ahead.

"At last!" Chrissy sighed. "I thought we were on the road to nowhere. That must be the hunting lodge. I hope."

The girls could see straight ahead of them, at the edge of a forest stood a large rectangular shaped house. It had four windows, all the same size on the top floor. On the bottom floor were four windows and a large front door with a small porch. Three chimneys ran along the top of the roof, one at each end and one in the middle. In the front of the house was a garden. The grass looked as though it needed cutting and the flowerbeds weeding. The road ran along-side the house and the garden.

As the girls approached the lodge they could see a man in the garden. He was stooped over an old push lawn mower. Chrissy thought the man was probably in his early sixties, as he looked like her grandfather, who was that age. She also concluded that this man was more than likely Harry Langford.

"Good afternoon sir," said Joan politely, as she got off her bike at the garden gate.

"Good afternoon ladies," replied the man. "Are you lost? We don't see many strangers up here."

The man's voice was very posh which implied that he had been given a good education and had a privileged upbringing.

"I think we might be," explained Joan. "We are looking for the old hunting lodge that used to belong to Kirkby Manor."

I understand what Joan is up to, thought Chrissy.

She probably doesn't want to appear to be nosey. "We are looking for Mr. and Mrs. Harry Langford," said Chrissy who had decided that she better get in on the conversation. "We heard they used to be the owners of Kirkby Manor and we are doing a school project on Kirkby Manor and its former owners."

"You have come to the right place then," said the man. "I am Harry Langord. How can I help you?"

"We were wondering if you could tell us a bit about your family?" asked Joan. "And about your way of life when you still owned the manor, that's if you don't mind Mr. Langford?"

"Well, we will see what we can do," replied Harry kindly. "Why don't you bring your bikes into the garden and come into the house with me. I will introduce you to my wife, Alice."

After doing what Harry had suggested Joan and Chrissy followed him round to the other side of the house, where they entered through a large wooden porch which was attached to the back door. This led into a short passageway and then into the kitchen.

The kitchen was a warm and inviting place, even though the yellow walls needed the plaster patching in places and a fresh coat of paint. The furniture in the kitchen consisted of a very large wooden Welsh Dresser that stood against the wall to their left. On the shelves of the dresser were an assortment of plates of varying shapes, sizes and designs. The dresser took up most of the wall on that side of the room.

In the centre of the room was a long wooden table, which was well worn but scrubbed very clean. Directly in front of them, against the back wall was a large porcelain wood burning Aga. It had six burners on the top and two ovens underneath. Chrissy remembered her grandparents having an Aga similar to this in their old farmhouse kitchen.

Harry ushered the girls to the door to the right of the Aga.

"Would you like to come through here ladies?" said Harry. "My wife Alice is in here on the couch. Unfortunately she is not very well these days."

He gently tapped on the door and then entered the room. The girls followed and closed the door to the kitchen behind them.

"We have visitors, my dear," announced Harry. "Two young ladies from the village would like to know a bit about the family. They are doing a school project on the past owners of the manor."

"Hello there, do come in and sit by the fire, it's very chilly in this old house," said Alice Langford, in a weak but welcoming voice. "It's lovely to meet you. We don't get many visitors, do we Harry?"

Alice was lying on a worn red velvet couch in front of the fire. She was a fragile looking creature who looked like she would break like porcelain if she fell. But she had a kindly face and a warm smile and although she now was showing her years in age through the lines on her face, her former beauty could still be seen.

"Do forgive me for not getting up," she said. "I'm afraid I can't walk well these days, I seem to spend endless hours on this couch."

The girls walked over to Alice and politely shook her tiny, bony hand and then settled themselves down on a large ottoman by the side of the fire.

As soon as everyone had settled, Joan told the Langfords about their school project. She told the story so well that even Chrissy started to believe that the phony school project was real.

"I'm afraid our family history as owners of the manor came to a very sad end," said Harry, when Joan had finished her story. "Do you know anything about our family?"

"We heard you had a brother Mr Langford?" enquired Joan.

"Yes, I did he died a number of years back now."

Harry seemed more sad than angry at the memory of his brother, even when he told them the story of how his brother Jack came to lose his claim to the manor and its lands. He wasn't even angry when he told the girls about the missing treasures from the house, which everyone thought Jack had taken.

What a nice old gentleman, thought Chrissy. "We are hoping our nephew Peter and Jack's wife Mary are still alive," said Alice, sadly. "But we have no idea where they would be living. We haven't heard anything from them or about them for many years."

"We would love to know where they are," announced Harry. "They are the only family we have left. That's if they are still alive."

Harry and Alice looked at each other sadly as they took hold of each other's hands.

"I hope this will be a good story for your project," said Harry regaining his composure. "Even though it's a bit of a sad and, unusual story."

"You don't mind if we write your story, do you?" asked Chrissy.

"Not at all, every family usually has some skeletons in their closets," laughed Harry. "Most of the local people know the story anyway. Now what else can we tell you?"

"We were wondering if you still had any of the old furniture from the manor house that we could take photographs of?" asked Joan. "And do you still have any of the old paintings or valuables from the house. Or any photographs of these pieces?"

"And do you have old jewellery that had been handed down to you by the family, Mrs. Langford?" asked Chrissy.

"I'm afraid not," explained Alice. "Everything of any real value was taken, even my beautiful diamond and ruby necklace and, earrings. Harry's father gave them to me after Harry's mother died. I had helped nurse her when she was very sick. She was a lovely lady."

"I remember dear," pondered Harry, "you used to wear the necklace and earrings to nearly every ball. You always looked so beautiful in them my dear. Then they disappeared with the rest of the valuables."

"Do you remember, Harry dear?" said Alice, with a smile on her face. "Your great Aunt, who had originally owned the necklace and earrings, was a Lady in Waiting to Queen Victoria."

"Yes I remember, my precious," said Harry affectionately. "And do you remember that very large, ornate candelabra that used to stand on the table in the dining room."

"Oh yes! That was your favourite piece."

"Yes, it was, my dear." Harry's voice held a note of sadness. "It had been given to Sir Percival Langford, many, many years ago."

"So you don't have any photographs of these things?" asked Joan.

"No, I'm afraid not," replied Harry. "But wait a minute! They have an archive up at the manor. We asked if one of the rooms could be kept for an archive when we sold the manor. It holds records and documents on the history of the family. We are a very old family and we owned the manor for a very long time. They will have some photographs there."

"That would be very helpful" announced Chrissy. She tried hard not to show too much enthusiasm, but this was very exciting news and probably would help them a lot.

"Thank you for your time, Mr. and Mrs. Langford." Joan got up from the ottoman and Chrissy followed. "We should be able to put together a very interesting project from what you have told us."

"You are very welcome, my dears," said Alice. "Can we see the project when you have finished it? We'd love to see you both again. Wouldn't we Harry?"

"Of course," replied Chrissy. "It may take a while to finish it though."

Chrissy thought they had better find the missing treasure pretty quick if they were going to find it at all. She would hate this sweet old couple to think they had been lying about their school project, for no good reason.

"I could see you were having trouble with your lawn mower, Mr. Langford," Chrissy enquired.

The thought had suddenly come to Chrissy that she could probably help Harry Langford out in the garden.

That way she could visit them more often without it being about the phony school project.

Chrissy was developing quite a fondness for the Langfords. With the fondness came a strong feeling of compassion for their loss and loneliness. Compassion was a feeling that was quite new to Chrissy. In the past Chrissy had only liked, loved or didn't like people. Now she was really feeling for them. Also, Harry and Alice Langford reminded her of her grandparents. She had been very close to them but they lived quite a distance away from her now. They moved away when they had sold their farm and retired.

"Yes, I find I can't manage the garden very well now," explained Harry. "I have quite bad arthritis. It's the damp in this old house. I am afraid we can't afford to have the outside walls damp proofed and re-plastered."

"Maybe I can come over and help after school, while it's still light," said Chrissy. "Then when it gets dark early I can come on Saturday afternoons until the winter. Then the grass won't need cutting for a while anyway."

"That's very nice of you, young lady. That would be very helpful."

"And you can stay and have some cake and a cup of tea with us afterwards," said Alice enthusiastically. "It would be lovely to have the company. We don't see many people up this way."

"I'll come some afternoons as well," interrupted Joan who didn't want to be left out. "That's when I don't have to help my mother!"

"That's settled then. I'll come on Wednesday," announced Chrissy. "If that's okay with you and, my dad, Mr. and Mrs. Langford?"

Alice Langford clapped her tiny hands together. She smiled up at Chrissy. A tear came into Chrissy's eye. She had made someone happy. This revelation made her feel happy and warm inside.

"By the way my dears, we know you are both from the village and we know you go to the local school but, we don't know your names yet," enquired Harry.

"I am Joan Parsons, and this is Chrissy Danvers.

You probably know my father Mr. Langford?"

"Of course, Edward Parsons, I've known him since he was a lad."

"We better be off then," announced Joan, who was still standing by the ottoman. "We will see if we can get into the manor archives before supper."

"Bye bye, my dears!" Alice waved to the girls as they walked out into the kitchen. "See you on Wednesday Chrissy."

"Do call us Harry and Alice," said Harry. "Mr. and Mrs. Langford seems so formal."

"It's not very respectful," explained Chrissy. "I was taught to be respectful to my elders. But maybe when we get to know each other better, I can call you Aunt and Uncle, if that would be all right with you?"

"Oh, that would be marvellous." Harry was quite taken with the prospect of being an adopted Uncle. "I haven't been called Uncle Harry since our nephew left."

The girls waved to Alice and followed Harry back through to the kitchen and out into the garden. They said their goodbyes to Harry and rode off on their bikes towards the manor house.

The journey wasn't too long but the girls found they only had just over an hour before the archives closed for the day and so they hurried on with their mission.

During their time in the large wood panelled room, which had most likely been the library, they found some very useful information that would help their investigations. This included photographs, one in particular of the ornate candelabra that Harry had described to them and another of the diamond and ruby necklace and earrings.

Chrissy could imagine the tiny Mrs. Langford wearing the jewellery and looking so beautiful dressed in fine clothes. She could picture her dancing round the ballroom at the manor, with all the well to do ladies and gentlemen of the county.

The photograph of the large ornate candelabra showed an inscription at the base of it. It was hard to read but it had writing on the back of the photograph. *This Candelabra was Presented to Sir Percival Langford for his devoted service to Prince Albert. 1861.*

The curator of the archives wouldn't allow any of the photographs to be taken away for copying and so the girls made sketches of the items they may find useful. And so with a feeling of accomplishment, Chrissy and Joan thanked the curator for his time and left for home. They now felt confident they would be able to identify some of the missing treasures, should they be fortunate enough to find them.

We will find the treasure, thought Chrissy as they cycled back to the village. I know we will.

CHAPTER SIX

The Mausoleum

It took a long time for Chrissy to get to sleep that night as the events of the day kept swirling round in her head. She was so excited about searching for the Langford treasure. She longed to find it and return the valuables to Harry and Alice Langford.

When she finally did fall asleep at a very later hour, she dreamt about the missing paintings, the large candelabra, and the man with the knife. The paintings were dancing about the churchyard and the man with the knife was chasing her. As he got closer she waved her arms about to defend herself. Then she felt something cold and smooth, it was the candelabra. She quickly picked it up to defend herself when suddenly something jumped on her.

Chrissy was woken from her nightmare with the feeling of something still on top of her. When she opened her eyes, to her relief she found it was just Smudge, her cat that had jumped on the bed.

"Oh, Smudge!" she gasped. "You gave me such a fright."

Chrissy looked at the clock, it was 9 a.m. and even though she still felt a little tired, she decided she better get up. Pushing Smudge onto the floor she dragged herself out of bed, put on her dressing gown, and walked downstairs.

The kitchen was empty, everyone must be out, she thought.

"It's Sunday what am I going to do today?" Chrissy said to Smudge, who had followed her downstairs. "We won't see Joan today Smudge, she has gone to visit her Aunt. I won't see her until tomorrow now. I'm on my own for the day."

Chrissy slumped down in a chair and drummed her fingers on the table. Smudge purred and rubbed his body round her legs. She bent down to stroke him and he purred even louder.

"I know Smudge," announced Chrissy. "I'll go up to the churchyard and have a look round myself. But I better not go until after the ten o'clock service. I'll leave here about eleven."

Smudge stopped and looked at Chrissy as though he was disapproving of the idea.

Who knows thought Chrissy, I may find some useful

clues or even some of the treasure.

"What do you think Smudge, shall I bring home that beautiful big candelabra?"

Smudge purred and rubbed himself round Chrissy's legs again. Her pyjama bottoms were now getting quite hairy from all the fuss.

"Come on Smudge, it's time for you to go out and catch some mice," announced Chrissy as she opened the kitchen door and gave Smudge a gentle push outside.

Chrissy made herself a hasty breakfast and ate it hungrily. After washing her dishes she ran upstairs to get washed and dressed. Then she looked at the clock again and found she still had another hour before eleven o'clock. Reluctantly she decided she better do some homework. Her decision to do this was made more out of a need to kill time more than out of enthusiasm to get her homework finished.

At eleven o'clock Chrissy put her homework away, put on her coat, and left the house for the churchyard. She took her time walking down the street. She didn't want to bump into anyone coming from the morning service, but as she approached the church she saw Reverend Timas standing outside. He was talking to a lady who was wearing a large feathered hat.

"Oh drat! I better go for a bit of a walk down Church Lane, to give them time to finish their conversation and leave," said Chrissy to herself.

It was a lovely sunny day. The leaves were turning all different shades of red, orange, and brown. The breeze blew some of the leaves off the trees. They fluttered down on Chrissy like large pieces of confetti. She was excited about the adventure she was about to go on, but content to be enjoying the countryside around her at that moment. She kicked at the fallen leaves and hummed her favourite *Beatles* tune.

Her feeling of contentment didn't last very long though. The minutes seemed to drag past until finally she decided it was probably safe to go back to the village.

When Chrissy arrived back at the church, no one appeared to be around. She quickly went through the porch gate and ran up the steps towards the church, but half way up she heard a car on the road below. She crouched down behind the wall that separated the steps from the steep bank and the road below.

She remained silent in her hiding place holding her breath until the car had passed by. Then she made a mad dash up the remaining steps and pressed herself flat against the church wall, so she couldn't be seen from the street below. She was out of breath she was shaking and had to pause for a moment. She then edged her way along the wall to the front of the church where the large stained glassed window hung. There she stopped to have a look round.

Chrissy's attention became focused on the small mausoleum which stood several feet in front of her. She knew these small stone buildings were burial chambers that held the coffins of the wealthy families of the district. Although this was now not a common practice, years ago each wealthy family had their own mausoleum.

Some of the buildings were quite decorative, like the one she was now looking at. The building was like a miniature Roman Temple. She had seen photographs of Roman Temples in one of her history books and could definitely see the resemblance.

Suddenly the sound of something moving through the woods behind the mausoleum caught Chrissy's attention. She hastily retreated back to the side of the church she had come from and pressed herself flat against the cold stone walls of the building and, waited.

She could hear a grating sound, like stone was being scraped against stone. Someone must be opening the mausoleum door. I wonder if it's our man from the shed, she thought.

Slowly she moved to the front of the church and into a position where she could observe the small building again. She crouched down so she would remain hidden.

It was the man from the shed. He was opening the door to the mausoleum. Chrissy could see he had with him the shovel and burlap sack from the shed. He also had a lantern.

When the man had the door open wide enough, he walked into the small building.

Chrissy waited a while to see what would happen, before she cautiously stood up to get a better look. But just at that moment the man walked out of the building again.

Her heart nearly stopped beating from fright. She crouched low to the ground, hoping that some of the gravestones in front of her would hide her from sight. She didn't move. She heard the door grating along the stones again and the sound of the man walking back into the woods. She waited a moment longer before she dared move from her hiding place.

The man was nowhere in sight and to her delight he had left the mausoleum door slightly open. She couldn't wait to satisfy her curiosity. Cautiously she made her way up to the small building. Then she walked up to the door and peeked through the crack but she couldn't see anything.

Chrissy checked to make sure the man was not returning and then she pulled the door open a little wider, but she still couldn't see anything. So she pulled the door open even wider until it was open wide enough for her to get body through the opening. Before she knew it, she was inside the building.

It was cold and musty smelling inside. Chrissy

sneezed and then quickly put her hand over her mouth.

Whoops! Someone might hear me, she thought.

She squinted as she peered into the dim light until her eyes gradually got accustomed to the dimness. She could see rows of stone shelves all round her, on her right, on her left and in front of her. On every shelf lay one or two coffins. Except for the shelf on the bottom row directly in front of her it was completely empty!

I wonder whose mausoleum this is, she pondered. There must have been a lot of them and they must have been rich. This building is quite fancy.

Just as Chrissy was about to walk over to one of the coffins to read the name on it she was startled by a rustling sound behind the building.

Without thinking she ran further into the chamber towards the far wall. She crouched down in a corner and held her breath just as the man from the shed walked into the room. He stood for a moment and scratched his head.

"I thought I closed the door more than this," said the bewildered man.

He looked round in the dim light then looked down to make sure the sack, the lantern, and the shovel were still where he had put them. He then picked them up and put them close by the door, along with something he took from his pocket. He took another look round the building again before he walked out and pushed the heavy door closed.

"Oh my goodness!" gasped Chrissy. "I've been shut in!"

She started to panic and tried to push the door open, but no matter how hard she pushed she hadn't the strength to move the heavy stone door. Exhausted and frightened she sat down on the cold stone floor.

"What am I going to do," she sighed. "I don't like the idea of sitting round here with these dead people for company, whoever they are."

Once again Chrissy tried to push the door open, and again she sat back down on the ground exhausted.

"Wait a minute the man has left the lantern with the shovel and sack." Her voice echoed. "He must be coming back later. Maybe after the six o'clock service, it will be getting dark by then."

Oh dear, she thought. I don't want to stay here until then, and I'm pretty sure my room-mates don't want my company either.

She made a further futile attempt at the door but again she sat back down on the ground exhausted.

"The lantern, maybe I'll try lighting the lantern. In

the Girl Guides they say if you rub two stones together they make a spark. Maybe that might have been a box of matches the man threw down by the lantern. If I get that lit at least it won't be so dark and spooky in here."

She fumbled in the darkness near the door. Her hand touched the lantern, she then grasped hold of a small box. She shook the box, she was right, it was matches.

She grabbed the lantern and fumbled with the matches to light the lantern. It took several attempts but finally she had it lit and a warm light illuminate over the small chamber. This made her feel more at ease.

Chrissy could now see that the coffins on the shelves were as decorative as the outside of the building.

I must see whose remains are lying in these coffins, she thought.

She walked over to the coffin on the lower shelf to her right and leaned over to read the nameplate. It was dusty so she had to wipe the plate with the sleeve of her coat.

"Edward Langford. 1867 to 1936." Chrissy read out loud.

"This must be the Langford's family Mausoleum," she shouted with delight. "How interesting and what a coincidence."

She knew that Edward Langford was Harry and Jack Langford's father. She must see more of the coffins. She leaned over to the coffin next to Edwards. It was *Sarah Langford. 1875 to 1930.*

"This must have been the wife of Edward and the mother to Harry and Jack," announced Chrissy.

Now she was really curious. Carefully she stepped on the shelf on which Edward Langford's coffin lay. She stretched up to read the nameplate on the coffin above. Again she had to wipe the nameplate with the sleeve of her coat.

"Agatha Langford. 1842 to 1912," she read. "I wonder if this was Jack and Harry's grandmother. Oh boy, she was seventy when she died. I bet she was a feisty old thing."

The coffin beside Agatha was Charles. 1837 to 1900. She assumed he must have been Jack and Harry's grandfather.

Chrissy was really excited about the discovery of the Langford family. She decided she had to see more and climbed to the shelf above Agatha and Charles. But on her way up to the next shelf she didn't realise she had accidentally moved Agatha's coffin out from the shelf at an angle.

Chrissy had to climb right up onto the top shelf and stretch so she could read the inscription on the coffin.

It was, *Sir Percival Langford. 1810 to 1868.*

Then disaster struck. Just as Chrissy had finished reading the nameplate on Sir Percival's coffin she lost her balance. She desperately tried to hang on to whatever should could, but in doing so she moved Sir Percival's coffin to the edge of the shelf. She couldn't stop herself from falling and on her way down she dislodged Agatha's already badly balanced coffin.

Chrissy fell with a thud to the ground with Agatha's coffin close behind her. The lid slipped off the coffin and as it came down off the shelf, Agatha's bony remains fell on top of Chrissy.

"Yuk! No thank you Agatha, I don't think I want a hug from you right now," gulped Chrissy in disgust, as she moved Agatha's bony arm from across her chest.

Chrissy shuddered and stood up to dust herself off but as she was dusting herself off disaster struck again. She was dusting off her hair and she had raised her hand too high. Before she realized what she had done, she heard the creaking sound of Sir Percival's coffin moving from the top shelf.

She screamed and tried to move out of the way, but it was too late. She was knocked to the ground by Sir Percival's coffin falling on top of Agatha and herself.

CHAPTER SEVEN

Little White Lies

Chrissy opened her eyes. She had a terrible headache. Faces were peering down at her. She jumped. She thought it was Agatha and Sir Percival coming to seek revenge on her for disturbing their peace.

She screamed. "Go away, I didn't mean to disturb you."

Chrissy! Chrissy! It's all right. It's me, Dad." Sam Danvers helped his daughter to sit up. "You're on the couch in the living room at home."

"What happened to you? Reverend Timas found you unconscious by the church door." Said Joan, as she appeared in front of Chrissy and knelt down on floor beside the couch.

Chrissy looked at her father. "I don't really know what happened. I must have fallen and knocked myself on the head or something. Maybe on the stone steps," she lied.

"What were you doing up at the church on Sunday afternoon, Chrissy? There is no service on Sunday afternoons," enquired Sam.

"Oh, errh. Oh yes! I went to see Reverend Timas about choir practice," Chrissy lied again. "I wasn't quite sure about this song we are supposed to learn. You know the one I mean, Joan?"

"Oh right. Yes. That song," Joan lied.

Chrissy looked at her father. "Dad, I feel a bit faint.

Could you get me a glass of water, please?" "Okay, dear, now you just lie still."

When Sam had left the room Joan hastily began questioning Chrissy.

"Chrissy, what really happened to you?"

"Do you remember at the front of the church, where the stained glass window is? There's that mausoleum a few yards away from the church," explained Chrissy. "Well, I got trapped in that mausoleum."

"What! What were you doing in there?" Joan cried. "I saw the man from the shed open the door to the mausoleum and go inside." Chrissy continued. "He came out a short time later and left the door open a bit. So I went to have a look. Well, you know me, I ended up inside."

"That was brave of you, wasn't it?" said Joan, sarcastically.

"Silly of me because the man came back a short time later. I was scared to death. I had to hide at the back of the mausoleum so he wouldn't see me. Then when he left for the second time he closed the door behind himself. It was shut tight."

"That was really stupid of you to go in there by yourself, Chrissy. But how did you end up by the church door, unconscious?"

"I don't know. Anyway, when I had recovered from the shock of being locked in that place I lit the lantern the man had left. Then my curiosity got the better of me and made me look at the names on the coffins, to see whose they were," explained Chrissy. "And you know what, Joan? That mausoleum belongs to the Langfords."

"Really!" Joan said with excitement. "Yes, isn't it exciting?"

"But I still haven't figured out how you ended up by the church door, unconscious," stated Joan.

"When I was looking at the names on the coffins, I dislodged one of them. It fell on top of me. The lid had come off when it was falling and Agatha's skeleton fell on top of me."

Joan shuddered at the thought.

"Well, after I managed to get Agatha's bony remains off me, I stood up to brush myself off, and while I was doing that I must have dislodged the coffin on the top shelf. It came crashing down on me. It must have knocked me out. I think our man from the shed must have found me and put me by the church door. He's probably not altogether ruthless."

"Oh, Chrissy, you shouldn't have been investigating by yourself. Who is Agatha, anyway?"

"Shhh! I can hear my dad coming," whispered Chrissy. She lay back on the couch with her arm dramatically draped across her forehead.

"How are you doing my little princess?"

Sam walked back into the room and handed Chrissy a glass of water.

"Oh, I'll be all right I think, Dad," moaned Chrissy weakly, as she continued her dramatic wounded soldier act.

"Chrissy, I have got to go out and feed the cows," said Sam. "Would you mind staying and watching her for a while, Joan?"

"Of course I will, Mr. Danvers."

Joan was eager to find out more about Agatha.

"Chrissy's sisters will be home soon," said Sam.

"And I won't be long. Chrissy, the doctor said you have to rest and keep quiet for twenty-four hours at least, so no excitement."

"I'll make sure she stays quiet Mr. Danvers," said Joan.

As soon as Chrissy's father had left the room, the girls resumed their conversation.

"Chrissy, you have to promise me you won't go off by yourself, ever again," demanded Joan. "You could have been killed, or you could have been left unconscious in that mausoleum for days. You would have suffocated and died."

"Okay, okay!" shouted Chrissy. "It was a frightening experience being left in there with the dead Langfords. Especially having Agatha Langford draped across me and then Sir Percival's coffin knocking me out."

"Oh, it was Agatha Langford, in the first coffin," said Joan.

"Yes!" said Chrissy, impatiently thinking that Joan

should have known it had been Agatha Langford in the coffin. "The thing is I am now wondering if the treasure might be hidden somewhere in or, around the mausoleum. If that's the case, our man is very close to finding it."

"I never thought of that, we have to do something quick. But you can't move for twenty-four hours. Oh, what are we going to do?"

"We need to lead him off on a false trail," announced Chrissy, as she put her hand to her head. "Ohh! My head."

Chrissy laid back. She really did feel faint now. "You know what the doctor told your dad, don't get too excited," scalded Joan. "You are right, though. We have to lead our man off on a false trail so that we can have a good look round the mausoleum ourselves."

Chrissy's head hurt even more when she tried to figure out what they could do.

"I've got it," announced Joan. "I will borrow some of my mother's silverware. She has a lovely old silver teapot, cream jug and, sugar basin. I don't have to let her know and we can have them back before she misses them."

"What for, don't you think your mother would be pretty upset if she found out?"

"My mother won't find out. They are kept in a

cupboard and only used for best and we haven't got any for-best-people coming over in the near future."

"I do hope you're right, Joan."

"What I thought we could do is use them as a decoy to lead our man along a false trail. I would lay them partially hidden in the grass, on a trail that could lead to another location, somewhere else in the churchyard."

"There is that mausoleum at the other side of the church," said a now excited Chrissy. "The one that's near the bell tower, we could lead the false trail to that one."

"Good idea. I could leave the silver cream jug near the Langford's mausoleum, the sugar-bowl a bit further on towards the other mausoleum, and the teapot outside the other mausoleum."

"Brilliant idea Joan! The only thing that worries me is when and, how are we going to lay this false trail? It will have to be soon."

"Tomorrow, straight after school, I can't do it before then. You won't be up until Tuesday and I will have to lay the trail myself."

"I could be up tomorrow," moaned Chrissy.

"No, Chrissy, take it easy. It's best to rest now and get over your knock on the head. If you get up too soon you could be laid up for days and we've got things to do.

Okay!"

"Okay but just be careful tomorrow. We don't want anything happening to you."

Chrissy was concerned about Joan being by herself. She didn't want her to be in a dangerous situation like she herself had been in.

"I will be careful, and I'll come and see you straight after I've done the job," said Joan. "My mum is out and dad watches a TV programme in the sitting room on Sunday nights. I'll sneak into the dining room and get the silver out of the cupboard tonight."

"You will come and see me straight after going to the churchyard," pleaded Chrissy. "Won't you?"

"Yes, I will. I'll tell my mum tonight that I am visiting you straight after school tomorrow. But of course, I will sneak up to the churchyard first, before I come to see you. There shouldn't be anyone around at that time in the afternoon and I should be able to get the job done pretty quickly."

"Let's hope our man's not around," said Chrissy, as she suddenly sat upright and listened. "I think my sister, Elizabeth, has just got home. I heard the kitchen door close. We better not say anymore."

"You're right. I better be off home, it won't be the same at school without you tomorrow. But I'll see you tomorrow afternoon, like I promised, as soon as I have finished in the churchyard."

"You make sure you're careful and keep your eyes open for our mystery man," warned Chrissy. "We don't want both of us laid up. I'll see you tomorrow."

Joan hurried out of the room. Chrissy sat upright again. She could hear Elizabeth talking to Joan.

"Hello Joan, and what's Miss. Mischief been up to now?" asked Elizabeth.

"She had a bit of a fall. Look, I must rush. I'll see you later."

Chrissy could hear the kitchen door open and close. She swifly lay back on the couch.

"And what have you been up to mischief?" asked Elizabeth as she entered the sitting room.

"Dad will tell you all about it," moaned Chrissy. "And don't call me mischief, Lizzie."

"Don't call me Lizzie, then," snapped Elizabeth angrily. "I hate that name."

"I won't call you Lizzie if you don't call me mischief, is that a deal!" Chrissy snapped back.

"Okay, a deal. Now tell me what happened?" asked

Elizabeth.

Chrissy lay back on the couch again, with her arm across her forehead.

"Oh, Elizabeth," moaned Chrissy. "You will have to ask Dad, I really do feel ill. Do you think you could help me up to my bed?"

"Okay Muffin," said Elizabeth kindly using the pet name she had for her sister.

Chrissy detected a different tone in her sister's voice, as she helped her to her feet.

Chrissy was glad of her help because she really did feel faint. Her legs felt wobbly, like jelly, especially when they walked up the stairs. She was relieved when they got to her room and she was able to lie back on her bed and let Elizabeth tuck her in.

"I'll come and check on you in a bit, Chrissy." Elizabeth went to the door and turned off the light.

Chrissy panicked. She didn't want to be left in the dark. She kept thinking of that cold, dark mausoleum.

"Elizabeth! Elizabeth!" She screamed. "Please leave the light on for me."

The distress in her sister's voice was obvious to Elizabeth. She tried to console her.

"Okay Muffin, if that's what you want. I'll see you in a bit."

When her sister had gone downstairs Chrissy lay in silence. The mausoleum and the dark and the dead Langfords had frightened her much more than she realized. She was afraid to go to sleep in case she had nightmares, but no matter how hard she tried, she couldn't keep her eyes open.

She fell into a restless sleep. She could see the skeletal remains of Agatha Langford coming towards her.

"You hurt my arm, you naughty girl," moaned Agatha.

Agatha's arm was hanging loose at the elbow.

A moment later, Sir Percival appeared out of the darkness. He was carrying the large candelabra.

"I'm sorry," screamed Chrissy. "I didn't mean to hurt your arm Mrs. Langford. I'm sorry for disturbing you. Please go away. Please go away, both of you."

She screamed again. "Chrissy! What's the matter?" Sam hurried into the room.

"Oh Dad, it was a bad dream," cried Chrissy as she snapped out of her nightmare.

"Look dear," said Sam. "I'll go and get you a nice cup of tea and then I'll sit with you for a while, until you go to sleep."

"All right, Dad. Thanks!"

Chrissy had decided to take Joan's advice. She had made up her mind up never to go on any more adventures by herself, ever again.

After a nice hot cup of tea and comfortable that her father was close at hand was Chrissy able to fall into a peaceful sleep. She was exhausted and slept peacefully until the morning.

CHAPTER EIGHT

An Amazing Discovery

It had been a long day for Chrissy. She hated being away from school and her friends. It was so quiet at home during the day and the only living things she had seen was Smudge and her father, who had come to check on her every now and then. Smudge was too busy chasing mice and her father was too busy repairing machinery in the barn for them to visit for long.

It was now five o'clock in the afternoon. Chrissy tried to read for a while to keep her mind occupied while she waited for Joan, but she couldn't concentrate.

She should have finished laying the false trail in the churchyard by now, thought Chrissy.

She tried so hard to keep her mind on the book but she just couldn't concentrate.

Finally at five-thirty, Joan arrived.

"At last I thought something might have happened to you."

"It's all taken care of," explained Joan. "The decoys are set in place and the false trail is laid."

"What a relief. Did you see anyone?"

"No not a soul! Well, not a living one anyway," Joan laughed.

"Very funny," said Chrissy sarcastically, who felt jealous because she had missed out on the action.

"I better be going, Chrissy. I'm sorry I can't stay long, but my mum will wonder where I have got too. I was in the churchyard longer than I expected. I'll see you tomorrow at choir practice. We have an extra practice this week, remember. Will you be up to it?"

"I'll be up to it even if I have to drag myself there. It's been a boring day. I only saw Smudge and my dad and that wasn't too often.

"Are you going to be able to go to school tomorrow?" asked Joan.

"Dad says I should stay at home one more day. But I will persuade him to let me go to choir practice, because it's so important and we have to practice the new hymn."

"We should meet early," explained Joan, as she was walking out of the room. "Then we can check to see if our man has taken the bait and been led off on the new trail. See you tomorrow Chrissy."

After another long day by herself Chrissy couldn't wait to get to the church that evening to meet Joan.

"You're in a hurry, aren't you lass," said Sam. "I've never seen you this keen to get to choir practice before."

"It's been boring at home on my own Dad. It'll be nice to get out, even if it's just to choir practice."

"Are you sure you are all right now?" "I'm fine now thanks. I'll see you later."

Chrissy hurried out of the house and down the street. She arrived at the church porch gate to find Joan already waiting for her.

"Come on, Chrissy. We have got to see if our man has taken the bait before the vicar gets here."

"I'm right behind you."

The girls raced up the church steps and hurried to the back of the church.

"He's taken the bait," shouted Joan excitedly.

"What about your mother's silver?"

She was concerned about Joan getting into trouble. This really was a new Chrissy. The feelings of concern for other people were even amazing herself.

"Don't worry, we'll get them back. I'm sure we're close to finding the Langford treasure."

"Look! It looks like the door to this mausoleum has also been opened. There are scrape marks on the stone floor," explained Chrissy.

They approached the mausoleum they had used to lead the man on the false trail. "It worked, your bait worked, Joan. You're brilliant!"

"That just proves that he is looking for the Langford treasure. That's why he took my mum's silver pieces."

"I'm going up to the Langford's tomorrow to cut their grass, like I promised," said Chrissy. "Do you think you can get away straight after school on Thursday? We can check out the Langford's mausoleum then. Time is running out. We have to see if we can find something soon that might help us find the treasure."

"I'm sure I can. Hey, we better get back down the hill to meet the vicar. He'll wonder what we've been up to up here, if he gets to the church porch gate before us."

The girls made it back down to the gate just before Reverend Timas arrived.

"Hello ladies," said Reverend Timas. "Are you feeling better then Christine? Are there just the three of us then again tonight?"

"Yes, just us Reverend Timas, and yes, thank you I am feeling much better," replied Chrissy.

She was trying hard to keep up with the vicar who was already halfway up the steps.

When the three of them were settled in the church, Chrissy found it hard to focus. She tried to keep her thoughts on the vicar and what he was saying, but her thoughts wandered in other directions. Her eyes carelessly searched round the church. For what, she didn't know. Then suddenly, out of the corner of her eye she saw a flickering, bright light. It was coming from *The Lady Chapel* that was situated at the far left of the main hall of the church.

"Reverend Timas!" screeched Chrissy.

"What now, Christine?" snapped Reverend Timas impatiently. "You're not day dreaming again, are you?" Chrissy could now see that the flickering light was a small fire that was burning against the back wall in *The Lady Chapel*. This was an area of the church that was used for small family Christenings and Weddings.

"Look!" screemed Chrissy.

She pointed to the spot where the fire was burning. "Oh dear! Oh dear!" squealed Reverend Timas.

"It's a fire."

Reverend Timas snatched his cloak from the back of the pew next to him and followed the girls who were already running towards the fire.

He beat at the flames with his cloak in an effort to put the fire out.

"Oh dear! Oh dear!" he cried. "I knew the old electrical wiring in here would cause problems one day."

Finally, the vicar got the fire under control and Chrissy could see he was exhausted after his valiant effort. What a scare, she thought. Reverend Timas was right something had to be done about the old electrical wiring in the church before something even more serious happened.

Even though Chrissy had done nothing to help put the fire out, she too felt exhausted from the excitement. She fell back against the wall behind her. Suddenly, to her surprise just as her body touched the wall she heard a rumbling sound that appeared to be coming from beneath her feet.

She jumped away from the wall just as one of the large stone blocks in the floor right in front of her slowly moved back leaving a large opening in the floor.

"What in heaven's name is this?" cried Reverend Timas.

Chrissy and Joan knelt down to look into the hole.

"There are steps leading down into what looks like a tunnel, Reverend Timas," observed Chrissy. "It appears to be a secret passage running under the church."

The vicar knelt down beside the girls, peering into the darkness.

"How amazing," exclaimed Reverend Timas. "What a discovery. I didn't know there were any secret passages in this church."

"Can we go down there?" asked Joan with excitement.

"No! No! Not now," said Reverend Timas hastily. "It's too late and it might not be safe down there. I must look into the old church records, to see if I can find anything out about the secret passage."

"But, Reverend Timas," Chrissy appealed. "We have to investigate soon. Someone might find out about the passage and go down there before us."

Chrissy was secretly worried that their man from the shed might find the secret passage and go down before them. The treasure might be down there.

"What are you babbling on about Christine? Who could possibly find out about this passage? No one I know has ever talked about it and there's only the three of us here tonight?"

Reverend Timas was puzzled by Chrissy's sudden anxiety.

"What I mean is," Chrissy tried to explain. "Joan and I would love to investigate the secret passage before anyone else does. We are doing a project at school on local history. This would be a very interesting topic for our project. Wouldn't it Joan?"

Chrissy was lying about phony school projects again.

"Yes Reverend Timas," agreed Joan. "We could get top marks for this one."

School projects to the rescue again thought Chrissy.

"I have to find out more about the passage first," Reverend Timas explained. "Like I said, it might not be safe."

At that moment a brilliant idea came into Chrissy's mind.

"Reverend Timas, while you are finding out about the secret passage, maybe you would let my father take us down there. He used to be a coal miner before he became a farmer. He is used to going down into dark, dangerous places. We can take lanterns and wear hardhats like the coal miners do," offered Chrissy.

"Please, Reverend Timas!" begged Joan. "It would be so exciting to go into a secret passage that perhaps no one has been into for centuries."

"Well, let me think about it. Maybe I should go in

there with you," suggested Reverend Timas.

"Oh no, Reverend Timas!" said Chrissy and Joan. "You would get awfully dirty."

What a feeble excuse, thought Chrissy. But they had to put the vicar off. Like she had thought earlier, the secret passage could be a key clue to solving the mystery of the missing Langford treasure. They had to be sure either way. Maybe that's why their man from the woods had been searching the church. The bell tower was behind the back wall of *The Lady Chapel* where the fire had started.

"You are two very eager young ladies," said Reverend Timas. "And you really think this would help you with your school project?"

"Yes Reverend Timas," replied the girls in unison. "All right then, maybe we could meet here Saturday afternoon, if your father is free, Christine?" asked Reverend Timas. "You can go down into the passage then. Meanwhile, I will see what I can find in the church records about this place. But please, ladies, make sure you bring torches and hardhats."

"We will! We will!" shrieked Chrissy.

"Now ladies, I think that's enough excitement and choir practice for one night. We just have to find out how to close this opening so no one else discovers it, or falls into it. Then we should all go home. And ladies, we should keep this to ourselves for now. Except of course for your father, Christine."

"We will, Reverend Timas," said the girls.

Chrissy and Joan proceeded to feel along the back wall of *The Lady Chapel*, where Chrissy had been leaning. They realised it must have been one of the stones in the wall that had opened up the stone in the floor, so they pushed on every stone, until they found the right one. The vicar then pulled a pencil out of the pocket in his robe and marked the corner of the stone with an "X".

"I will tell the ladies not to waste their time cleaning in here on Thursday night," explained Reverend Timas. "I'll say it's not been used for a while, so it doesn't really need it, which is true. Christine, can you go and get me the lantern?"

The vicar lit the lantern and instructed the girls to wait by the main entrance to the church, while he turned off the main electrical power switch.

When the vicar returned they walked out of the church, locked both the doors, and walked down the steps to the road in silence.

"Well, ladies, I will see you on Saturday afternoon, shall we say two p.m.," shouted Reverend Timas as he headed off in the direction of the vicarage. "If it's convenient for your father, of course, Christine, let me know if it's not."

"Yes Reverend Timas we will," muttered Chrissy. "Goodbye, we will see you on Saturday," shouted Chrissy and Joan.

Chrissy couldn't wait for the vicar to be out of sight so she could talk to Joan.

"What do you think," gasped Chrissy. "I bet this is what the man has been looking for in the church. He must know something about the secret passage. He must think it's somehow connected to finding the treasure."

"I think you're right and I think we should try and investigate the passage ourselves before Saturday afternoon."

"How?" asked a puzzled Chrissy.

"Remember the vicar said the cleaners are in on Thursday evening this week," Joan recalled. "My mum usually sends flowers for the church alter arrangements. Maybe I can ask if we can take the flowers up to the church for her."

"I see. Then we can investigate the passage on Thursday night. But how are we going to do that with the cleaners there?"

"When the cleaners are doing the flower arrangements at the alter, you can keep watch and I'll go down into passage," explained Joan.

"I don't know if that's a good idea, Joan. It might not be safe for you to go in there by yourself. You know what you said to me about investigating by myself."

"I won't be by myself," said Joan. "You'll be keeping watch for me. Before we give the flowers to the cleaning ladies, we'll secretly get the vicar's lantern from the church porch and hide it in *The Lady Chapel.* Then I will have a light when I go down into the passage."

Chrissy still wasn't convinced that it was safe for Joan to go into the passage alone but Joan talked her round to the idea. Chrissy knew there was no time to waste. Their mystery man from the shed would realise soon enough that he had been following a false trail. "What about our plan to look round the Langford mausoleum on Thursday afternoon?" asked Chrissy. "We should still do that. Every clue or scrap of evidence we can find to help us find the treasure is important."

"So on Thursday afternoon we'll see if we can find clues round the mausoleum and on Thursday evening you will go into the passage?" asked Chrissy.

"Yes! I'll see you on the school bus tomorrow." "Bye!" said Chrissy. "I'll see you tomorrow."

As usual, Joan was already half way down the street.

Chrissy was so excited, she felt pretty sure they would find something on Thursday. They might even find the treasure itself.

She skipped across the road to her house. She felt like she had wings on her feet. She couldn't wait.

CHAPTER NINE

The Search Continues

After school that Wednesday Chrissy went to Harry and Alice Langford's, to cut the grass and do some weeding in the garden. Afterwards, they all enjoyed a hot cup of tea and a slice of fruitcake and had a nice chat.

The three of them discussed the school project. Chrissy told the Langfords that she and Joan had found some very useful information in the archives at the manor and that their school project should get top marks. She hated lying to the Langfords about their phony school project. But she knew it was important to keep quiet about their investigations, even though she was dying to tell them about the mausoleum and the secret passage.

Straight after school that Thursday the girls went home to change. They met at the church gate half an hour later.

"You were quick," said Chrissy. "I thought I would

be here first."

"No one was home at my place so I was able to hurry without anyone disturbing me," explained Joan. "Come on, let's get going. I have to be home by four-thirty."

"Did you talk to your mum about taking the flowers up to the church tonight?"

"Yes. I spoke to her yesterday. She was quite pleased I offered because she has a Women's Institute meeting tonight. Did you talk to your dad about going into the secret passage on Saturday?"

"Yes, he was very interested."

The girls had a quick look round to make sure no one was watching them, before they ran up the church steps. Then with their backs to the church wall, they made their way round to the front of the building where they could see the Langford mausoleum.

Joan whispered. "You know something I never noticed this building before. It's quite fancy, isn't it?" "Yes, the Langfords must have been really rich at one time," deduced Chrissy.

The girls took another look round the churchyard to make sure their mystery man was not about, then made their way over to the mausoleum.

"Right," said Joan. "Let's see if we can open this door."

Joan ran her fingers round the edge of the mausoleum door.

"I've no idea how the man opened it, I didn't see. Let's try pushing on some of these bricks in the wall, to see if one of them opens it." Chrissy suggested.

The girls pushed on every brick round the door of the mausoleum but, it didn't open. Chrissy then spotted a brick that was sticking out from the wall a bit further than the others. She pushed on the brick and the door of the building slowly creaked open. It opened just enough for them to put their hands through the opening.

"Well! Aren't you a clever Dick," said Joan, sarcastically.

"Nothing surprises me anymore. I have also come to the conclusion that the world is full of mysteries, like the vicar said."

Joan pulled the door of the building fully open and peeked inside.

Chrissy stood back. She was remembering being shut up in the mausoleum and the coffin falling on top of her. It felt like the hairs on the back of her neck were standing on end. Beads of sweat formed on her forehead.

She must pull herself together, she thought. Joan was with her. Nothing was going to happen to her.

"I can hardly see a thing," muttered Joan as she tried to see into the darkened room.

The sound of Joan's voice made Chrissy jump. She had not been concentrating on what had been going on around her. She pulled herself together as she realised they had work to do. They had to find the Langford treasure to help Harry and Alice.

Joan observed the floor of the mausoleum when her eyes became accustomed to the dim light.

"It looks like whoever carried you to the church door also cleaned up after you as well. Although there's still a lot of dust and stuff on the floor, all the coffins are back on the shelves."

"Our mystery man appears to be quite a considerate man in a sinister way," muttered Chrissy. "First he carries me to the church door, so someone will find me. Then he puts Agatha's bones back in her coffin and puts her back on her shelf. He also put Sir Percival back on the top shelf."

He must be awfully strong to do that, thought Chrissy.

"He certainly does seem to be a bit of a mystery," Joan agreed. "I wonder why he's looking for the treasure."

"I wonder. If I didn't know he had a big knife hidden

in the shed I wouldn't have minded meeting this man," said Chrissy.

"He hasn't left his lantern in here, has he?"

Chrissy ran her fingers across the floor just inside the mausoleum. Her hand touched something odd. She was curious to see what it was, so she picked it up and lifted up to her face so she could see it better.

"Oh yuk!" shrieked Chrissy. "It's a bone! It must be one of, Agatha's."

She quickly dropped the bone back on the floor and looked at Joan. Joan was doubled over and shaking uncontrollably. She thought there was something wrong with her until she saw Joan was laughing.

"Oh Chrissy," laughed Joan. "Anyone would think you just got hold of Agatha's arm again."

"It's not funny," retorted Chrissy, trying to stop herself from laughing too. "You didn't have Agatha's bones lying on top of you."

"Okay, point taken. Anyway, how on earth are we going to see in here?" Joan laughed.

"How about we go and get the vicar's lantern from the church porch," suggested Chrissy.

"We can't silly, the church porch is locked." "Well,

time is getting on," muttered Chrissy impatiently. "I think we better just stick to searching the passage tonight. If we find nothing there we can come back here tomorrow afternoon, with a lantern."

"Good idea," Joan agreed.

Chrissy could see Joan was still laughing. She pushed her to make her stop but she started laughing herself. Tears came into her eyes from laughing so hard.

"Oh come on Chrissy, we better close this place up before Agatha decides to come out of her coffin again. Ohhh!" spluttered Joan.

"Shut up, you."

Chrissy quickly closed the mausoleum door and made a mental note of where the stone that had opened the door was.

"Let's have a quick look round the outside," announced Chrissy, as she made her way to the back of the mausoleum. "Look! It looks like our man has been digging round here. The grass has been cut away and then loosely put back."

"The walls must go down quite deep beneath ground level," said Joan, as she moved some of the earth back from the building. "He's dug down about four feet and you can still see the bricks of the wall that far down."

Chrissy looked into the hole.

"I wonder what he was hoping to find."

After looking round the remainder of the building and finding nothing more interesting, the girls made their way back down to the road and headed for home.

"I'll see you about six o'clock," shouted Joan as she left Chrissy outside her house. "I'll come and call for you. It doesn't matter if anyone knows we are taking flowers up to the church for my mum."

CHAPTER TEN

The Secret Passage

Chrissy and her father were sitting at the kitchen table talking about the secret passage, when at six o'clock precisely, Chrissy heard a knock on the kitchen door.

"I'll get that," said Sam as he got up to open the door.

Joan was standing on the other side of the door holding a very large, colourful bunch of flowers.

"Oh how nice to see you Miss. Parsons," said Sam. "You've brought me some flowers."

"Oh no Mr. Danvers," cried Joan. "They are for the church."

"I know, don't worry," laughed Sam. "Won't you come in?"

Chrissy giggled.

"He fooled you," she laughed.

"No. I'll not come in thanks, Mr. Danvers. We better be going or the cleaning ladies will be finished, before we get these flowers up to the church. Are you ready, Chrissy?"

"Goodbye Miss Parsons, next time will you bring me some flowers?" said Sam grinning.

"Of course Mr. Danvers," laughed Joan. "Goodbye."

Chrissy grabbed her coat from a hook by the kitchen door.

"I'll see you later Dad. We might visit Sarah Richardson after we have taken the flowers to the Church. I'll be home about eight."

"Don't be much later than that Miss, you have homework to do and school tomorrow."

"Okay, Dad," said Chrissy as she rushed out through the door before her father could say anything else.

When Chrissy and Joan arrived at the inner porch to the church, Chrissy reached up to the ledge where the vicar kept his lantern and matches. She stealthily opened the door and peaked round inside.

She whispered to Joan.

"The cleaning ladies are up at the front pews. I'll sneak this lantern over to *The Lady Chapel* before they come back down here. You wait here by the door just in case they look this way."

It excited Chrissy that she was the one making the decisions for a change.

"Hurry up," whispered Joan.

Chrissy tiptoed over to *The Lady Chapel* and put the lantern behind the last pew closest to the entrance of the passage. She could just make out the vicar's pencil mark on the stone that opened the entrance to the passage.

Silently she tiptoed back to Joan.

"When you have given the flowers to the ladies," she whispered. "Tell them you will get the vases from the back of the church. But instead of getting the vases, sneak over to the Chapel and open up the secret passage."

"Okay, that's a good idea."

"When you don't come back straight away, I'll say I wonder where Joan has got to, and I'll pretend to go and look for you. When I come back down this way you go into the secret passage. I'll get the vases and take them back to the ladies. Then I'll come over to the entrance of the passage and keep watch. I'll crouch down behind the pews so no one will see me."

"Your brain's working overtime today Chrissy and you are getting bossy too."

"That makes a change, me being bossy instead of you."

Chrissy made a funny face at Joan and pushed her to the front of the church towards the cleaning ladies.

"Hello Mrs. Smedley," said Joan. "My mum sent me with the flowers today."

"How lovely," said Mrs. Smedley. "A lovely colourful bunch of flowers as usual. Are they from your mother's garden?"

"Yes! Why don't I get the vases from the back of the church for you to put them in," suggested Joan.

"Thank you, dear that's a good idea."

"And how are you, Christine?" asked Mrs. Smedley.

"I'm very well thank you!" replied Chrissy. "Are you well yourself."

"Very well, thank you dear."

"The church looks lovely and clean."

Chrissy tried to make conversation with the ladies to

keep them occupied while Joan opened up the entrance to the passage. She could hear a faint rumbling sound coming from the back of the church. It must be the stone in the floor rolling back, she thought. She coughed to cover up the sound.

"Oh dear, I've got a tickle in my throat. Maybe I should get a glass of water from the back of the church. I'll see where Joan has got to with those vases as well."

"Good idea," said Mrs. Martin, who was helping Mrs. Smedley. "We don't want these lovely flowers wilting, do we?"

Chrissy made her way back down the aisle. She looked behind her to make sure the ladies weren't watching her and then she hurried across to the Chapel and the entrance to the passage.

Chrissy whispered down the hole in the floor. "Are you all right down there? Can you see anything?

"Yes, I'm all right," replied Joan in a muffled voice. "And no I can't see anything unusual, just an awfully long passage."

"Be careful," whispered Chrissy. "Are you sure you should be down there by yourself?"

"I'm alright, just keep watch."

The muffled sound of Joan's voice came up through

the hole in the stone floor.

"I'm just taking the vases to the cleaning ladies and then I'll be right back," whispered Chrissy.

Chrissy got the vases from behind the organ at the back of the church and filled them with water from the sink at the bottom of the bell tower. She looked up into the tower. She remembered for a moment how their adventure had started just a few days ago.

When she returned to the front of the church with the vases she was relieved to see that the cleaning ladies were still busy in the same place as they were when she had left them. She briefly spoke to them. Put the vases on the alter and hurried back to the Chapel.

She was worried about Joan being in the secret passage on her own. She had a bad feeling about the whole situation. Maybe it was because she was remembering being trapped in the mausoleum.

Chrissy realised there was not much she could do now but be there for Joan. She sat herself down on the cold stone floor behind the pew next to the entrance of the passage and waited.

It seemed like she had been waiting for hours and there was no sign of Joan returning. Chrissy was starting to get worried. She chewed nervously on her fingernails when suddenly she felt a rumbling underneath her. A small cloud of dust came out from the entrance of the passage.

Oh no! What has happened? She panicked. She imagined having to tell Joan's parents that Joan was trapped in a secret passage under the church. What would they think? What would they say? Joan could be dead and she would be grounded for life.

"Oh where are you Joan?" pleaded Chrissy down the hole. "Are you alright?"

She peeked over the top of the pew to make sure the cleaning ladies were still busy and then she whispered down the hole again.

"Joan! Joan! Are you alright?"

She nervously peered down into the darkness. She could only see to the bottom step but beyond that, it was complete dark.

Oh no, thought Chrissy. What has happened, I can't even see the light from lantern.

Then she heard a faint coughing sound in the distance.

"Joan! Joan! Are you alright?" Chrissy asked anxiously.

She tried to keep her voice as quiet as possible.

A few moments later Joan appeared at the bottom step of the entrance to the passage. She was covered in dust. The lantern was in her hand but the light was out.

"What happened?"

Joan climbed up the steps and sat on the floor. She still held the lantern in one hand, but her other hand was on her head. A trickle of blood was oozing out from underneath Joan's hand.

"You're hurt," cried Chrissy. "What happened?" "I was a few yards into the passage," muttered Joan in a voice that seemed to belong to someone else. "When my arm caught on something sticking out from the wall. Before I knew what was happening part of the roof of the passage caved in on me."

"Oh Joan!" wailed Chrissy. "I knew it was too dangerous for you to go in there by yourself. I had a bad feeling about it. The whole lot could have collapsed on you."

Chrissy pulled Joan's hand away from her head. "That's quite a deep cut. Come on, we better get that checked out. I'll take you to my place. We are going to have to tell my father. We'll have to tell him everything. It's not safe to search that passage, without someone with us, who knows what they are doing."

"It's okay. Before the roof came down, I saw what looked like the entrance to a room. It was just a few feet in front of me."

"You're kidding!"

Chrissy was now very excited.

"I think we are onto something," stated Joan. "I really think we are on the right trail. So, you see it's alright to tell your father now. I saw this with my own eyes this is not your vivid imagination. He has to believe that we are onto something."

"Come on Joan. Let's close the entrance and get going. I've got to get you to my place before anyone sees us and wonders what you have been doing to get so dusty and cut up. We'll tell my dad the whole story and get him to get us back down here as soon as he can."

Chrissy found the stone in the wall that closed up the entrance to the passage then stood up to check where the cleaning ladies were. They were still busy at the front of the church arranging the flowers for the alter.

With a bit of luck they should be able to get out of the church without being seen, thought Chrissy.

She took Joan by the arm and led her to the church door. They managed to get through the door without being noticed. She got the matches and lantern from Joan and quickly put them back in their place on the shelf in the porch. She then led Joan out into the fresh evening air.

Chrissy didn't feel safe until they had gone down

the church steps and had made their way down the road to her house. They eventually got to the safety of her kitchen and to her own warm safe surroundings.

CHAPTER ELEVEN

Confessions

Chrissy sat Joan down at the kitchen table. Then she took a tea towel out of the drawer by the sink, wet the towel under the tap and handed it to Joan to put over the cut on her forehead. Then she went to find her father.

"Dad! Dad!" Chrissy shouted. "Can you come here, please? Joan has been hurt."

Chrissy returned to the kitchen a short time later with her father.

Sam looked at Joan curiously.

"What on earth happened?" He said. "You're covered in dust."

"Dad," Chrissy pleaded. "Can you just have a look at the cut on Joan's head. Then we'll tell you everything."

Joan moved the damp tea towel away from her head

to show the cut to Chrissy's father.

"It's a bit of a nasty cut," said Sam. "But I don't think you'll need stitches. I'll clean it up and put a plaster on it."

"Thanks Mr. Danvers," murmered Joan.

"Why didn't you take Joan straight home Chrissy?" asked Sam as he reached for some disinfectant and cotton wool from the cupboard.

"I couldn't Dad. We'll tell you why in a minute." "Between the two of you, you've certainly been getting into some scrapes just lately. Something fishy is going on here," remarked Sam as he finished cleaning Joan's wound. "I'll just run upstairs and get a plaster. Then you better tell me what's going on. Okay?"

Yes Dad," said Chrissy obediently.

She knew she was going to be in deep trouble if they didn't tell the whole story. She just hoped her father would believe them.

"Are you alright now Joan?" asked Chrissy when her father had left the room.

"Yes, I'm fine. I don't think it was anything big or heavy that fell on me."

When Sam came back into the kitchen and had put

the plaster on Joan's wound, he motioned Chrissy to sit down next to Joan. He then sat down at the kitchen table opposite them.

"Okay girls," he said. "Out with it and don't miss anything out."

Chrissy told her father the whole story. From the time they saw the shadow in the bell tower, to the shed in the woods, old Tom's story about the Langfords and their search of the mausoleum. Also how Chrissy got trapped in the mausoleum, right up to the discovery of the secret passage and the events of that evening.

After she had finished she saw a look of disbelief on her father's face. He sat speechless for a while.

"Is this the truth, Joan?" Sam finally asked. "I know my daughter has a vivid imagination. I certainly hope you haven't."

"It's true Mr. Danvers," explained Joan. "I wasn't in the mausoleum with Chrissy, but I believe her story about what happened to her there. I did say to her that she shouldn't have gone into the mausoleum by herself."

"No, she shouldn't have," snapped Sam.

Chrissy noticed a severe look of disapproval on her father's face.

"I know for a fact everything else is true because I was

there and I don't have a vivid imagination Mr. Danvers."

"Chrissy said you told her, before part of the roof caved in on you that you thought you saw what looked like a room or a chamber a few feet ahead of you in the passage. Are you sure about this?" asked Sam.

"Yes! It was definitely an opening. I really do believe we are onto something and that we might find the treasure down there."

Joan was now getting excited.

"Just think, Dad," interrupted Chrissy. "How much it would help the Langfords if we found their lost treasures."

"We can even identify some of the treasure. We saw pictures of some of the items up at the manor," said Joan.

"I have drawings of those items," added Chrissy her enthusiasm growing by the minute.

"I have to admit, it is quite a story. But I am inclined to believe you. I agree it would help the Langfords if we found the treasure."

"So are you going to help us Dad?" pleaded Chrissy. "Yes! I'll help. Look it's getting late. You better be going home soon, Joan. Your parents will be wondering where you are."

"What am I going to tell them about the cut on my

head, Mr Danvers?" Joan asked.

"I hate to tell you to lie to your parents, but this time I think you'd better. For the moment anyway," explained Sam.

"Tell them you tripped and fell when you were coming out of the church."

"I think we better try and dust your clothes off a bit first," said Chrissy. She was looking at Joan's shabby appearance.

"Yes," said Sam. "You'd better wash your hair as well. It's full of dust. Chrissy has a hair dryer so you can get it dry quickly. Go upstairs you two and wash Joan's hair, Chrissy. But first, bring Joan's jeans and jumper down here. I'll dust them off as best I can."

"Oh, Mr. Danvers," said Joan gratefully. "You're a lifesaver."

The girls ran upstairs to the bathroom. Joan took off her jeans and jumper and Chrissy took them downstairs to her father. She then went back to the bathroom to wash Joan's hair.

"You're dad is so understanding," said Joan.

Joan now had her head bent over the bathroom sink as Chrissy washed her hair.

"My parents would have gone bananas."

"Yeah Dad can be pretty cool sometimes," said Chrissy, proudly.

"I don't think my parents would have believed our story. When are we going to go back down into the passage? It's got to be soon or our man from the shed might find out about it and go down there himself."

Chrissy listened and thought as she briskly rubbed Joan's hair with a clean towel.

"Be careful, Chrissy," Joan cried. "You are not drying your dog, Skeffy. You are drying me and you are hurting me."

"I'm sorry," said Chrissy. "I am used to drying the dog. Dad has to wash him quite often because he's always going down rat holes."

"I'm just going to get my hairdryer from my bedroom. You finish rubbing your hair to get it as dry as possible."

Chrissy threw the towel to Joan and ran to get her hairdryer. She then took Joan into her bedroom and dried her hair.

"You're right," said Chrissy getting her thoughts back to the Langford's treasure. "We shouldn't wait too long before we go back into the passage. I was thinking of asking my dad if he would phone the vicar tonight and find out if we can go into the passage tomorrow after school. Do you think you'll be able to get away from home tomorrow afternoon, after school?"

"I should be able to."

"I'll get dad to tell the vicar that he can't go down into the passage on Saturday because he is very busy," Chrissy continued. "I'll get him to say that we are really excited about going into the passage so we can get on with writing about it for our school project."

"Christine Danvers, you really are starting to think for yourself. I'm proud of you and I'm sorry I called you bossy earlier on. I don't know what I would have done today without your help.

Chrissy gave Joan a big hug.

"You're my bestest friend ever," she said bashfully.

"And you're mine," said Joan, grinning.

It wasn't long before Joan was dressed again and looking more presentable. She didn't look like a poor, dirty, little urchin from the street like she had done earlier. Her clothes had been briskly brushed and her hair was clean and free of dust.

The girls hugged each other again.

"I'll be off then. See you, Mr. Danvers," shouted Joan

as she hurried out the door. "Thanks for everything." "Bye! Bye! Now don't go tripping up on the way home and mess yourself up again." Sam laughed.

"No Mr. Danvers, I'll see you later."

Chrissy closed the kitchen door and followed her father into the living room.

"Dad?" said Chrissy, as she settled herself on the couch. "I think we should go back into that secret passage as soon as possible. We don't want our mystery man from the woods discovering the treasure."

"You're probably right. When do you suggest we go? You sound as though you have this all planned out."

"You don't think it's too late to phone the vicar tonight, do you? You can ask him if we can go down there tomorrow afternoon, after school."

"I'll try him. I'll say I can't make it on Saturday and that the two of you are excited about going into the passage because you want to include it in the school project that you have to have finished soon."

"Great minds think alike Dad," Chrissy laughed. "That's just what I thought you could say to him."

Sam picked up the telephone in the living room and dialled the operator to get the vicarage. Whe the vicar answered the telephone, Sam explained the situation and stressed the urgency of Chrissy and Joan's request.

"That's very good of you, Reverend Timas, the girls will be very pleased. They are very excited about this project."

There was a pause in the conversation. Chrissy saw her father nodding his head.

"Really!" continued Sam. "That is very interesting. Yes, I will tell the girls."

Chrissy couldn't wait for her father to get off the telephone and tell her what was so interesting.

"Okay, Reverend Timas," said Sam continuing his conversation with the vicar. "We'll see you about four tomorrow afternoon then."

Chrissy impatiently tapped her feet on the floor.

She was dying to know what the vicar had said.

"Yes. I'll bring the hard hats and lanterns. I've extra hats for the girls. Good-bye Reverend Timas, and thank you again."

"Tell me what's really interesting, Dad?" said Chrissy, impatiently when her father had put the telephone down.

"Reverend Timas said he thinks the secret passage was built in the mid-fifteen hundreds, when Mary Tudor was on the throne. Have you covered the Tudors in history, yet?" he asked.

"We've just started on the Tudors."

"The history books say the Catholics wanted to get their lands back from the Protestants. It was the land that had been taken from them when Mary Tudor's father Henry VIII formed the Protestant church."

"Why?" asked Chrissy.

"It's a long story and you'll be coming to that in your history lessons soon. Anyway, when Mary Tudor came to the throne she reinstated the Catholics. She was still a faithful Catholic herself, like her mother had been. So in turn the Catholics recovered much of their land back from the Protestants. Reverend Timas believes that the secret passage was built for the Protestant clergy to escape if they needed to."

Chrissy sat and listened intently to her father. She was now looking forward to learning more about the Tudors. History was her favourite subject at school.

"Our church is still a Protestant one and as you know, it's now called, *The Church of England.*"

"All reigning monarchs of England become the head of the church. This was something else that was brought about by the Tudors."

"That's pretty interesting, Dad," said Chrissy. "I can't wait to learn more about this in my history class. Isn't it exciting the secret passage could be hundreds of years old."

"Yes, it could be. So, Chrissy Danvers, your wish is granted. Reverend Timas will let us go into the secret passage tomorrow. As long as we are properly dressed, wear hard hats, and have lanterns. Now, young lady go and do your homework."

"Thanks, Dad."

Chrissy hugged her father.

"I really hope we find the treasure tomorrow." "So do I, for the sake of Harry and Alice Langford, although I've never met them, they sound like a deserving couple."

Chrissy ran upstairs to her room. She rushed through her homework. She was sure she did most of it wrong. But that didn't matter she would soon have an interesting and real school project to write about. That's if they found the treasure tomorrow. She was so excited.

When Chrissy finally got into her bed she found she couldn't get to sleep. Then when she did finally fall asleep she dreamt again, about the mausoleum and the secret passage. This time in her dream Agatha and Sir Percival were leading them into the chamber.

The whole chamber was full of treasure. The large

ornate candelabra stood in the middle of the room surrounded by valuable paintings, beautiful jewellery made with glittering diamonds, precious stones, and several other pieces of silver.

A smile came across Chrissy's face as she slept peacefully through the night.

CHAPTER TWELVE

The Secret Chamber

At three-thirty, that Friday afternoon, Joan knocked on Chrissy's door. Chrissy and her father were waiting in the kitchen.

They had everything ready for their expedition. The miner's hard hats were on the kitchen table ready for the girls to try on. Mounted on top of the hats were battery-operated lights. The lights enabled the miners to see underground without having to carry lanterns.

"Okay girls, try these on," said Sam as he handed the girls each a hat.

He adjusted the straps on each hat so they would fit securely.

"They feel awfully funny," mumbled Chrissy. "You have to wear them they protect you from anything falling and hitting you on the head, like what happened to Joan."

Chrissy took off her hat then got two large paper bags from out of a drawer in the kitchen and put the two hats in the bags. She didn't want anyone asking any questions about why they were on their way to the church carrying hard hats. Sam put his hat and the lantern in a rucksack and swung it over his shoulder.

"What else is in the sack Dad?" asked Chrissy.

"It has some emergency supplies in it in case we need them. I hope we won't though. Come on then, let's be off."

The three explorers arrived at the church at the same time as the vicar. Chrissy's heart pounded with excitement at the thought of a real life adventure.

"Are we all her then?" asked Reverend Timas. "Good! So let's go into the church and see what you can find in the mysterious secret passage. This is a very exciting moment, he added."

They followed Reverend Timas into the church and waited by the front door while he turned on the electricity.

A moment later a warm light spread throughout the building and the three explorers made their way over to The Lady Chapel where Reverend Timas was already waiting.

"Are we all prepared?" asked Reverend Timas. "Yes, I believe we are," replied Sam. "Test the lights on your hats girls. I'll light the lantern."

Reverend Timas pushed on the brick in the wall which opened the entrance to the passage. The stone in the floor groaned as it moved back to reveal the stone steps.

"This is quite a discovery." Sam's voice held an air of anticipation.

"This passage could be over four hundred years old and probably no one has entered it in all those years and now we are going down there to investigate where it leads too."

Very convincing Dad, thought Chrissy. Well, at least the vicar thinks no one has been down there for four hundred years.

The three explorers carefully made their way down the steps into the passage. Chrissy felt a little nervous about the unknown so she stayed close behind her father. Joan gladly followed in the rear.

"Mr. Danvers, what do we do when we get to the place where the roof caved in?" Joan enquired.

"I have a couple of small garden forks in my bag. If the cave-in isn't too bad they will help us to dig through. If it's bad we will just have to go back."

"Oh no Dad," moaned Chrissy. "We can't give up

now."

"Chrissy, I'm sure there will be some large spades somewhere in the church grounds. We can get them and come back."

"Okay!"

Chrissy could see that the walls, floor and ceiling of the passage were made of hard packed dirt supported by wooden beams. The whole place smelt musty and stale. It also felt cold and damp. She began to feel closed in.

There's not much air down here, thought Chrissy. I wouldn't like to have been an escaping vicar. I wonder where the passage leads too, it seems to be endless.

"The cave-in should be just round this corner," announced Joan, after they had gone several yards into the passage. "See! There it is."

"This doesn't look too bad," said Sam. "It looks like one of the wooden beams came loose. That's what must have hit you on the head Joan. We can soon prop it up and make our way through."

With the help of the garden forks, the three of them soon had the passage clear enough to pass through.

"Look there Mr. Danvers!" shouted Joan. "There's the room I saw before the roof caved in."

A few feet in front of her, on her left, Chrissy could see an opening in the passage wall and at that moment her excitement overcame her previous fears. As she walked closer to the opening, she could see that it was a small chamber.

Sam held the lantern up behind Chrissy as their eyes adjusted to the light. They could see the floor of the chamber was covered with shining objects.

"It must be the treasure," exclaimed Chrissy. "It is the treasure. We've found the treasure! We've found the missing Langford treasure!"

Chrissy could see large oil paintings, silver candlestick holders, candelabras, silver teapots, jugs, platters, goblets, and a wooden chest that was full of precious stones and jewels. There were necklaces, bracelets, and earrings. Their pecious stones shone brilliantly in the lantern light and just as Chrissy had dreamt the night before, there in the middle of everything stood the large, beautifully decorated candelabra that had been presented to Sir Percival.

"Oh wow! Isn't it all so lovely! "Chrissy screamed with delight.

Chrissy was now absolutely bursting with excitement. She walked into the room and touched everything. Her mouth was open in amazement.

The manor must have been a very magnificent sight

with all these beautiful things in it.

She could see that most of the oil paintings were of people. One might be Agatha, thought Chrissy. I'd love to see a painting of Agatha as she was before she became a pile of dusty bones.

Joan followed Chrissy as she made her way over to the chest that held the jewels. She opened a velvet lined box which held a diamond and ruby necklace and earrings.

"Look Joan, it's Mrs. Langfords missing jewellery, I would recognize them anywhere. Aren't they beautiful?"

She picked up the necklace and admired the glimmering stones. The diamonds and rubies shone brilliantly in the lantern light. She then placed the jewellery carefully back into its box and back in the chest with the other jewellery. She walked round the room in a daze and kept thinking of the Langfords and how much this was going to help them. She felt on top of the world.

All their questions and all their investigations had been worth the effort. After all these years they could finally return the lost treasures to their rightful owners.

"Chrissy!" shouted Sam suddenly. "Move away, the ceiling is coming down above your head."

The sound of her father's voice brought Chrissy out of her day dreams, she quickly moved without another thought. A large hole started to appear in the ceiling above where she had been standing. She stood back against the wall of the chamber with her father and Joan. No-one spoke.

The end of a rope came through the hole and hit the floor in front of them.

"Quickly," whispered Sam, as he turned off the lantern. "Turn your lights off."

"There's someone coming down the rope," whispered Chrissy.

They all watched intently as a light came through the hole. Then a person appeared through the hole, first their legs, then the rest of the body. A man slowly slithered down the rope. A lantern was attached to his belt.

It was the man from the woods. Chrissy recognised his tweed jacket. She stood frozen to the spot.

The man reached the floor, he hadn't seen them yet. He took his lantern from his belt and slowly moved it round the room. The treasure shone brilliantly, as his light shone over it. Then the light shone on the three explorers who were still standing like stone statues, with their backs against the wall. The man dropped his lantern, he looked shocked.

Sam quickly turned his lantern back on and told the girls to do the same.

Chrissy saw a look of horror appear across the man's face. Then the look turned into anger. She was frightened. She didn't like what she was seeing. She felt a shiver go down her spine. She really believed they were in danger.

The man pulled something out of his back pocket and pounced towards Sam. Chrissy could see the man had a knife. She screamed.

"Dad, look out! He has a knife!"

The man knocked Sam to the ground. There was a struggle as Sam tried to get hold of the knife but he couldn't get it.

Chrissy saw her father was in grave danger.

That man's going to stab Dad, she thought. What could she do? She grabbed the first thing she could get hold of. It was a large silver goblet. She rushed towards her father and the man. As soon as she could work out who was who among the wrestlers, she hit the man on the back of the head. He fell forward. He looked as though he was unconscious. The knife had fallen from his hand.

Chrissy was frozen in shock. She dropped the silver goblet. What had she done? Had she killed the man? Oh no! She didn't want to be a murderer.

"Are you alright, Mr. Danvers?"

Joan was kneeling beside Sam. He seemed dazed.

"Yes. I'm okay!" he said. "Thanks to Chrissy!"

Chrissy was dazed and scared. Joan and her father's voices seemed to be coming from a distance. She could feel someone shaking her, or was she shaking herself?

"Chrissy! Chrissy! Snap out of it," squealed Joan. "You're frightening me. You look as though you're in a trance."

"Come on, Chrissy," appealed Sam. "Snap out of it. Everything is all right."

"What about the man? I might have killed him. I'm probably a murderer. I didn't mean to hurt him. He was going to hurt you Dad."

"Don't be silly. I'm sure he's alright," said Sam. "Let's have a look at him."

Sam cautiously moved toward the man who was lying in a crumpled heap on the floor. He felt his neck and wrist for a pulse.

"He's still alive."

Sam gently straightened out the motionless figure. "I think he's coming round," moaned Chrissy.

The man slowly began to move, he put a hand up to his head. He appeared to be in pain and he looked dazed. Then he realised he was not alone. He quickly jerked away but the sudden movement made him fall back and wince in pain again.

"Don't be afraid," Sam reassured the man, as he went to help him.

"Who are you?" The man asked. "Why are you here?"

He looked at Sam, then at Chrissy and Joan.

"I know who you are," he said to Chrissy and Joan. "You're the two girls I've seen hanging round the churchyard. You're trying to steal my treasure, aren't you?"

The man appeared very agitated.

"What do you mean your treasure?" said Chrissy, angrily. "It belongs to Harry and Alice Langford."

"No it doesn't," said the man. "It was rightfully my father's. My mother and I suffered for years with little money to live on, after we had left my father because of his cruelty to my mother. This is rightfully ours."

"You're, Peter Cropston!" said Joan. "How do you know who I am?"

"We heard the whole story about you and your family from old Tom Peters," explained Chrissy. "And we heard that the manor and the contents were left to your Uncle Harry and Aunt Alice, not to your father. He stole those things."

The man hung his head. Chrissy thought he was going to cry.

"My mother is very sick," moaned Peter. "She suffered for many years while she brought me up by herself. She worked so hard doing any odd job she could find. It's not easy for a woman bringing a child up by herself. People look down on women working and bringing up their children by themselves. They wonder what type of family you came from and how you came to have the child in the first place."

"That's true, some folk are like that," interrupted Sam. "Some of our society still has a Victorian attitude."

"I've had odd jobs here and there," continued Peter. "But as soon as people found out we were descended from a rich family they didn't want anything to do with us. They thought we had done something bad and been disowned and disinherited by our family. My mother left my father because he was a bad person, not because she was a bad person."

"It wasn't your fault your father was bad." Chrissy felt sympathy for Peter.

"Your Uncle and Aunt tried to find you and your mother. They said that you're the only family they have left. They know your father's actions were not your fault."

Peter put his hand on his head. Chrissy thought he

was crying.

"You mean they don't hate us?" Peter said. "My mother will be so happy. She needs family now that she is sick and getting old. Her own family disowned us. They haven't had anything to do with us since we left my father."

The poor man, thought Chrissy. What an awful life they must have lived.

"I'm sorry I went after you with my knife, Mister," moaned Peter. "I was so desperate to find this treasure so that I could make life easier for my mother."

"My name is, Sam Danvers," said Sam introducing himself. "This is my daughter Christine and her friend Joan. They have been looking for the treasure for your Aunt and Uncle."

"Your Aunt is also very sick," explained Chrissy. "And your Uncle is suffering so badly with arthritis, he can't even write anymore. They live in the old hunting lodge that used to belong to the manor. They can barely afford to keep that place going as they have little money now, themselves."

"I heard they had to sell the manor house," said Peter. "But I didn't know they were also poor."

"I know your Uncle and Aunt want you to be part of the family again," stated Joan. "They told us they wanted to find you and your mother. We know they will help you both."

During the conversation, Chrissy heard a faint voice coming from down at the end of the passage near the church.

"Oh, Dad," she said, suddenly remembering the Vicar was waiting for them in the church. "I think the vicar must be getting worried about us. I can hear him shouting down the passage."

"Oh dear, I better go and tell Reverend Timas we're alright. Then I'll come back for you all. Can you stand up Peter?" asked Sam.

"Yes. I think so," Peter replied, as he shakily got to his feet. But he wobbled and put his hand to the back of his head, he had to sit down again.

"I think I'll sit down until you come back, Mr Danvers," groaned Peter.

"The girls will stay with you, I won't be long."

"As long as Christine, doesn't hit me over the head again!"

Peter managed a faint smile.

"Please call me, Chrissy," she laughed. "I promise I won't hit you again. I was just protecting my father."

"Well, if that's the way you protect someone, you can be my protector any time."

"By the way, where did you come down from?"

Chrissy asked. "What is above us?"

"It's the Langford mausoleum," explained Peter. "I had my suspicions the treasure might be in a secret room below it. I read about the church before I came here to search for the treasure. I read in an old history book that there was supposed to be a secret passage that ran under the church."

"I'm surprised that the vicar didn't know about it then," interrupted Joan.

"How did you find the secret passage?" Peter asked.

"By mistake, a fire broke out in *The Lady Chapel*. I accidently pushed on a stone in the wall and the entrance to the passage appeared in the floor." Chrissy said proudly.

"That was an unusual piece of luck," exclaimed Peter.

A short while later Sam returned. He told everyone that he had briefly explained everything to the vicar and that they would fill in the details later.

"The treasure will be safe down here until tomorrow," said Sam. "I'm sure no one else knows about this place.

Is it the mausoleum that is above us, Peter? Did you close the door?"

"Yes, it is the mausoleum and I did close the door."

"Come on everyone, let's get going then."

Sam helped Peter to his feet and let him lean on him as he led him into the passage.

"Dad, can Peter stay with us tonight?" asked Chrissy.

"Yes dear, if he wants to."

"Thank you, Mr. Danvers," said Peter. "It will be nice to sleep in a proper bed for a change."

"Wait a minute Dad," shouted Chrissy. "I just want to take Mrs. Langford's diamond and ruby necklace and earrings. I would like to give them to her personally."

Chrissy quickly picked up the velvet lined box and followed the rest of them into the passage.

When the four of them had climbed back into the chapel, Sam asked Reverend Timas if he would like to go back to their house. He deserved a cup of tea and an explanation of everything that had been going on.

Oh, what a story, thought Chrissy, as they all made their way back to her house. The vicar is hardly going to believe it.

CHAPTER THIRTEEN

You Shall Go To The Ball, Chrissy Danvers

When everyone arrived at Chrissy's house Reverend Timas was told all about the missing treasure and the story of the Langford's misfortunes.

Afterwards they all discussed the situation and agreed what to do next.

It was decided that in the morning, which was Saturday, Sam would drive Peter home to his mother, Mary. They would give her the news about the family and the missing treasure and then bring her back with them. It would be arranged that she and Peter would stay the night with Sam, Chrissy, and her sister, and on the following day, on Sunday, they would take Peter and his mother up to the Langford's house.

Chrissy and Joan's job was to cycle up to the Langfords in the morning, to give them the news of their relatives and the discovery of the missing treasure.

Reverend Timas had the task of finding some strong, trustworthy men from the village to go into the Langford mausoleum and bring up the treasure from the secret chamber. From there they would take it to the vicarage where Reverend Timas would list each item, with the exception of the chest that hel the family's jewels. The chest was to be taken up to the Langfords when Chrissy, Sam, and Joan took Mary and Peter Cropston to see their relatives.

When everyone was clear on what their specific jobs were to be, they all said their goodbyes and went home or to their beds.

Chrissy slept soundly that night, she had no bad dreams, just a peaceful, restful sleep.

The next day was a lovely sunny Saturday. Chrissy and Joan arrived at the Langfords about ten o'clock that morning to be greeted at the garden gate by Harry Langford.

"I saw you coming from an upstairs bedroom window," said Harry excitedly. "What a pleasant surprise and how lovely to see you both today, we weren't expecting any visitors."

"We have some news for you and Mrs. Langford," announced Chrissy who could barely contain her excitement.

"Well come in, my dears, let's go and see Alice."

The girls followed Harry Langford into the house and through to the sitting room where Alice was lying on the couch.

After all the hellos had been said and everyone was sitting down, with a nice hot cup of tea and biscuits, Chrissy began to tell the story.

She told the Langfords of all the events of the past couple of weeks and how they had found the missing Langford treasure, but she didn't mention the discovery of Peter and Mary Cropston.

"Well bless my soul," exclaimed Harry. "What wonderful news. Oh Alice dear, we can get the house repaired at last and you can get that expensive medicine we couldn't afford to buy. You will feel much better after taking that."

"Chrissy! Joan! You are two very special young ladies," Alice cried.

Chrissy could see tears in Alice's eyes. Wait until I tell them about Peter and his mother, she thought. Then I will give her back her diamond and ruby necklace and earrings.

"Did you find out who the man was that you had seen around the churchyard, the one who attacked your father Chrissy?" Harry asked.

"Yes we did and you wouldn't believe who he was!

It was none other than your nephew, Peter Cropston."

"He had also been searching for the treasure," Joan continued. "He wanted it to help out his mother. They haven't had an easy life since they left Kirkby Manor, all those years ago."

"Peter's mother is also sick," said Chrissy, sadly. "We are not quite sure what is wrong with her, but she can't work anymore."

"Oh dear me," said Alice. "How sad, we must see them, they must come here. They must come and live with us, there is plenty of room. Don't you agree, Harry dear?"

"Of course my dear, we wouldn't have it any other way."

"We thought you would want to see them," said Chrissy. "My father took Peter home this morning, to give his mother the news and bring her back with them. They will stay with us tonight. Then we shall bring them up here tomorrow."

"Chrissy and I can help you get their rooms ready for them this morning, if you like," said Joan eagerly. "Wonderful! Wonderful!" exclaimed Harry. "We really cannot thank you enough. Mary will be a lovely companion for Alice. I remember she was a sweet person and they used to get on wonderfully together.

Didn't you Alice dear?"

"Yes we did, she was a very good friend as well." "Yes," recalled Harry. "She was quite a few years younger than my brother. Back then she was too young to realise what my brother was like. He wasn't faithful to her."

"Harry dear, you shouldn't talk about things like that in front of the girls, or to anyone other than family," scolded Alice.

"Rubbish dear, the girls are old enough to understand and they are like family."

Harry gently reprimanded his wife.

Chrissy smiled. What a lovely thought that the Langfords thought of them as family.

"There is just one more thing, Mrs. Langford," announced Chrissy. "I thought you would like to have these now, instead of waiting until tomorrow when we bring back the jewellery chest."

Chrissy handed Alice Langford the velvet lined jewellery box. Alice opened it immediately. She could see tears in Alice's eyes again. They slowly trickled down her small, frail face. Tears came into her own eyes as she watched the old lady. It was such a wonderful feeling to think she and Joan had made the Langfords so happy.

"My beautiful necklace and earrings," Alice cried. "Look Harry, it's my necklace and earrings, the ones your father gave to me."

"Yes my dear, it is lovely for you to have them back and I promise you that you will have an occasion to wear them again very soon."

Chrissy and Joan helped Harry make up the beds in the spare bedrooms. They then said their goodbyes and promised to be back by 10 the next morning.

That evening, Joan had tea with Chrissy, her family and the Cropstons. At the beginning of the evening Peter gave Joan back her mother's silverware. It had been in the shed in the woods.

The whole party enjoyed a lovely tea and then chatted for the rest of the evening. They talked about the Langfords and the Cropstons, about the past, and the future. Sometimes they laughed at amusing things that had happened and at times they nearly cried. They talked until they were all tired, exhausted and ready for their beds.

It's been a long and very happy day, thought Chrissy, as she snuggled down in bed that night. She was sleeping in her sister Susan's, room, as she had let Peter have her room. Mary had the guestroom.

Chrissy had very pleasant dreams that night. She

woke up bright and early the next morning feeling refreshed. When she went downstairs she found everyone had started their breakfast already. They were to be ready to go up to the Langford's by ten o'clock.

Chrissy, Sam and Joan stayed with the Langfords for lunch which Harry had made, ready to heat up and serve before they arrived.

At lunch Harry told them all stories about the family when the old master, his father, was alive and about when everyone was happy, except for Jack. Chrissy felt she had known the family all her life. They now felt like part of her family.

"What a wonderful day it's been," she said to her father that night. "I'm sure I will sleep well again tonight. I had lovely dreams last night. It was the first time since I got trapped in the mausoleum that I've had good dreams.

That night, Chrissy had happy dreams about her mother and she was surprised that when she woke up she didn't feel sad. Although she knew she would always love and miss her mother, she had other people in her life now to love and care about. She also knew that she could see her mother whenever she wanted. What more could she ask for.

During the week, Reverend Timas had all the items from the chamber returned to the Langfords. He had arranged for a man to come and buy anything they didn't want to keep. He had also arranged for a builder to start repairs on the lodge, Peter was also able to help with some of the repairs.

Chrissy and Joan had gone up to the Langfords, after school twice that week. During their visits they found out that the family had received quite a lot of money from the sale of the items they had sold. They had sold most things, except for the candelabra, Sir Percival had been presented with and all of the oil paintings of the family. Chrissy was finally introduced to the portrait of Agatha Langford.

"She looks a lot better than when I last saw her." laughed Chrissy.

It had been a busy week and now it was late on Saturday afternoon and Chrissy had nothing to do. It had been over two weeks since she and Joan had started on their quest.

"It's so quiet," moaned Chrissy, to her father. "Where is everyone? It's going to be so boring round here, now we have solved the mystery and found the Langford's treasure."

"I'm sure you and Joan will soon find another mystery to get yourselves involved in," said Sam, with a worried look on his face. "But right now, I would like you to go upstairs and put on your best dress. I'm going to take you and Joan out for dinner."

"Ohhh! How lovely, Dad, where are we going?"

Chrissy asked. "Does Joan know we are going out? Can I put my best blue dress on?"

"It's a surprise where I am taking you and yes, you can put on your best blue dress. Joan knows we are going out and we are picking her up in about an hour."

Chrissy was ready in no time and before she knew it, she was in the car with her father and Joan. They were on the road at the end of the village, half way up the hill, when Sam turned off the main road, onto the road that went to the hunting lodge and the manor.

"Where are we going, Dad?" asked Chrissy. "Are we going to see the Langfords?"

"We can drop by and say hello if you like but I have to take something to Matron up at the manor, first."

Ten minutes later the car pulled up at the front door of Kirkby Manor. The place was all lit up like someone was having a party or a grand ball.

"Why don't the two of you come with me," suggested Sam as he got out of the car and opened the car doors for Chrissy and Joan to get out.

The three of them walked to the massive oak front doors of the main building and walked inside.

Where is everyone, thought Chrissy. Where are the elderly people who live here?

They followed Sam through the main entrance hall to the back of the building. Chrissy was getting really curious now about where they were going. They then approached two large carved oak doors and Sam opened them. He went inside the room. Chrissy and Joan followed.

Chrissy couldn't believe her eyes when she walked into the room. They were in what must have once been the ballroom. The room was full of people. Everyone was cheering and clapping. She could then see a long banner draped across the top of the stage at the end of the room. On the banner was written the words, *HURRAH FOR CHRISSY AND JOAN, THE WORLDS GREATEST DETECTIVES!*

Chrissy took hold of Joan's hand and walked forward. She was in a trance. All the people in the ballroom moved to the side to let them through.

As the girls approached the stage Chrissy could see the Langfords, Cropstons, and Reverend Timas on the stage. Alice Langford was sitting in a wheelchair. She was wearing a beautiful ball gown and her necklace and earrings.

"Come here my dears," said Harry Langford as the girls approached the stage. "Welcome to our grand ball, which is held in honour of you both."

"But, before we start the celebrations," Alice Langford,

interrupted. "Harry has a presentation to make."

Harry took an envelope out of his jacket pocket and gave it to Reverend Timas.

"Reverend Timas, my family and I are honoured to present you with this cheque. It is a donation made on behalf of Christine Danvers and Joan Parsons," Harry continued. "To pay for new electrical wiring to be installed in the church and when the work is complete, we wish you to put up this dedication plaque on one of the church walls."

Peter Cropston stepped forward with a wooden plaque but before he gave it to Reverend Timas he held it up for Chrissy and Joan, and everyone to read. It read: *THIS PLAQUE IS PLACED HERE IN HONOUR OF CHRISTINE DANVERS AND JOAN PARSONS, WITH MANY THANKS TO THEM FOR THE NEW ELECTRICAL WIRING IN OUR CHURCH.*

"At the bottom of the jewellery chest," explained Alice. "We found all the missing stocks certificates. They were still very valuable and we received a great deal of money for them when we sold them. There was enough for us all too comfortably live on and more. Our bank has made some very good investments for us, which will keep us financially comfortable without any worries."

"We have someone coming in to clean the house, so Aunt Alice and Mother don't have to worry about it," continued Peter. "Uncle Harry is going to research the family history and record his findings on audio tape for someone to write. I'm going to make the garden look beautiful again and paint. Two things I have always loved to do."

Chrissy could hear everyone clapping and cheering again. Tears flooded into her eyes. She had never felt so special and appreciated in her whole life. A warm feeling glowed inside of her. She and her best friend Joan had done something for some deserving people and because of that they had made those people very happy and gave them a better life. They had achieved something worthwhile.

She had everything she could ask for, the best father in world, the bestest of friends, a very special and loving family, and a newly found second family and all these wonderful people in the room from the village and surrounding areas, were her friends. She didn't need to take herself into her imaginary world anymore.

What more could Chrissy Danvers ask for, except maybe for another mystery to solve.

While waiting for the extraordinary Reveren Timas on Toggleton Common have
been seeing a fiery eyed, fierce looking creature coming out of the woods at the far
side of the common. The sounds coming from the beast are hideous and frightening.
It scares every creature away—animal and human.

After Chrissy and Joan see the beast for themselves, they decide to investigate.
Unearthing secrets concerning an old man living as a recluse in an old
farmhouse near the common and his son's disappearance over a year past
gradually come to light during their investigations.

Did the beast kill the boy? During their investigations Chrissy finds herself
in frightening and compromising situations which seem impossible to escape
from. Will they succeed in solving the mysteries?

J. P. Darcey was born in Lincolnshire, England, in 1953.
She moved to Canada in 1975 with her husband and two
young sons. She now lives alone in a remote part of County
Donegal, Ireland—a beautiful place that inspires her to write.
The Shadow in the Bell Tower is JP's first published novel.

J. P. has enjoyed writing from an early age and written poetry and short
stories. She also took a course through the Institute of Children's Literature
in the US, writing for children and teenagers.

Mysteries, murder, and detective stories are a prevalent genre, and J. P. has
natural talent for this kind of storytelling.

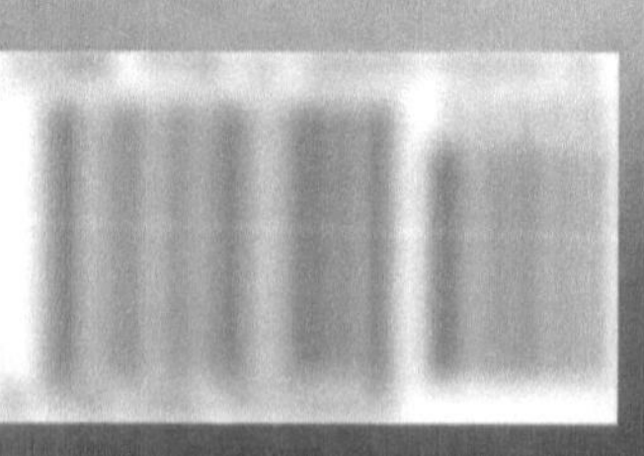